THE SHELBYDOG CHRONICLES
BY SHELBY COLE

THE SHELBYDOG CHRONICLES
BY SHELBY COLE

As Recorded by Mark G. Boyer

A Novel

RESOURCE *Publications* · Eugene, Oregon

THE SHELBYDOG CHRONICLES BY SHELBY COLE
As Recorded by Mark G. Boyer: A Novel

Resource Publications
An Imprint of Wipf and Stock Publishers
199 W. 8th Ave., Suite 3
Eugene, OR 97401

www.wipfandstock.com

PAPERBACK ISBN: 978-1-6667-6082-8
HARDCOVER ISBN: 978-1-6667-6083-5
EBOOK ISBN: 978-1-6667-6084-2

VERSION NUMBER 102622

Dedicated to
Janet Kubetschek,
proprietor of
Weston Pass Guest Apartment,
and Girlfriend, her dog.

"... [D]ogs say and think about so much more than we ever thought they could."

—Christina Hunger, *How Stella Learned to Talk*

"Part of our happiness experience comes from allowing ourselves to be in relationship with all of our own life experiences, without labeling them good, bad, or neutral. Just accepting them with love and maybe a bit of humor."

—Paul Sutherland, "Keep Meditating," *Spirituality and Health*

CONTENTS

ACKNOWLEDGMENT

WHILE THIS NOVEL IS fiction, there exists a non-fiction dog named Shelby, who is the inspiration for this book and who lives and travels with the author.

1

BIRTH AND PUPPYHOOD

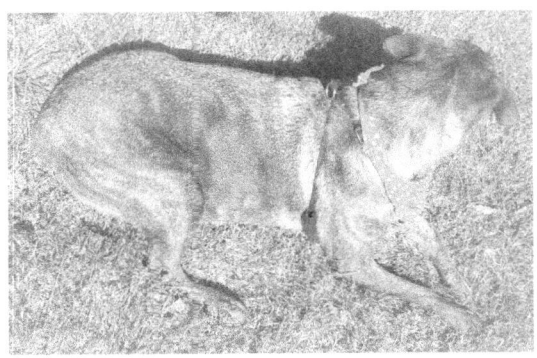

HELLO! MY NAME IS Shelby Cole. I used to have another last name, but I have long forgotten it. Furthermore, it brings back sad memories for me to even think about it. I would like to begin by telling you a little about myself. If you are wondering how I am able to type this without thumbs, I can't. Mark—otherwise known as Mark G. Boyer, my current owner—although I prefer to call him my friend—is typing this for me. Since I am bilingual, knowing both dog talk and English, and he is good at translating my dog talk into English when necessary, I have appointed him my secretary. Thus, while this book is about my life, in some way it is also about his; you see, our lives converge at this point in time.

A good place to begin is in the beginning. My mother was a Labrador, and from what she told me I have learned that my father was a Boxer—not the kind that puts on gloves and dukes it out in a ring! One day when my mother was in heat, the Boxer tricked the kennel worker and escaped from his cage. Before he could be caught, he had reached my mother and inseminated her. Two months later on April 7, 2012, my mother gave birth to six puppies arrayed in various furs colored in black and white—except for me: I was brindle from nose to tail. For those of you who don't know what brindle is, it is brown with cream streaks and red highlights. At one and the same time, I was a beauty and an oddity in the dog family. I had four brothers and one sister. Of course, at the time of our birth, I did not know that I had four brothers and one sister, and I did not know what their colors were or what mine was. It would be two weeks before I began to see a little, and two more before I could see clearly. It would also be two weeks before I could hear all the squealing and guttural growls that emanated from all of us. All I knew is that I was dropped from my warm, cozy place inside and near my mother's beating heart onto the floor, where I felt against me other wiggling puppies.

Very quickly our mother began to rub her rough tongue over me, removing a sticky substance that had gotten stuck to me. Of course, I couldn't see her; all I could do was feel her licking me clean and smell her. Then, she picked me up by the scruff of my neck and deposited me on the rug in her kennel. After cleaning my brothers and sister in the same way, she picked up each one of them and moved him or her to the same spot with me. And we made a pile of puppies! Then, she came and lay on the rug as close to all of us as she could get.

The next thing I remember is snuggling up to one of the teats on my mother's belly. I didn't know why I was supposed to do that—instinct I guess—but I did it. I could sense and feel and smell my brothers and sister attempting to do the same thing. With her nose mother pushed me closer to where I could grasp the teat with my lips. I presume that she was doing the same thing for my brothers and sister. As soon as I began to suck on the teat and push against my mother's belly with my little front feet, sweet, warm liquid flowed into my mouth, and I swallowed it. It made my stomach warm and comfortable and gave me a safe feeling. The heat of my mother's body also warmed me, while I sucked milk until I fell asleep. My mother, of course, continued to nose me and lick away any remaining afterbirth while I slept and my brothers and sister did the same.

The first two weeks of my life all I did was eat and sleep. I would wake up, scurry to find a teat, suck greedily, and fall asleep, slipping away from the source of my life for a few hours before I awakened and did it all again. Of course, not being able to see or able to hear made it difficult for my brothers and sister and me to scramble to mother and find a teat while rolling over each other and shoving each other out of the way. Smell was my main way of determining if I was going in the right direction to find food. Because all of us were born with four toes on four feet with each toe having a nail, it was not difficult to get a few scratches from time to time. When our area with mother got dirty from all the peeing and pooping that was going on when we were not eating or sleeping, she would pick up each one of us by gently grabbing the scruff of our necks with her teeth, carry us one by one to a new, clean location, deposit us where she wanted us, and go back and get the rest one at time. By the time she finished, we were hungry again and vying for positions on teats. By the end of our first week of life, we had each doubled our birth weight, give or take an ounce.

Lots of things continued to happen to my siblings and me. At four weeks, we began to grow dog baby teeth. That meant that the human woman, who took care of my mother, began to place a type of gruel mixed with milk on a saucer. I remember tasting it with my tongue, but decided that mother's milk was much better. Gradually, one by one my brothers and sister nibbled on it until the woman put more on the saucer, and we ate it. No one told us that we were now eating solid food.

With fully developed eyeballs around ten weeks old, all six of us were walking, stumbling, and wagging our tails. Being able to see, to hear, and to walk—not even mentioning following the smells our noses found—made it very hard for our mother to keep track of us. We might wonder away, get lost in the grass when we were outside, or forget where we were. Our baby teeth were gradually pushed out and our adult teeth came into our little mouths. This development made us want to chew on anything and everything we could find. Sometimes we chewed on the rug in our kennel. Outside we chewed on sticks. Sometimes our kennel keeper gave us milk bones to chew on—they tasted very good!

I remember one day when the kennel keeper put all of us puppies in a box and used it to lead our mother out of the kennel and into the grass that was just sprouting. I had discovered that I loved to explore. I would begin with a leaf and move on to a clump of wild garlic and from there to a small evergreen bush. As I sniffed from one thing to the next, I also moved farther and farther away. I was alone, and when I turned around, I could not see my mother, brothers, or sister. And I began to panic and to cry. My heart was pounding in my chest. I had been so focused on smelling everything in sight that I had lost focus of my mother and siblings. In just a few seconds, however, I saw my mother running through the grass to answer my cries. She stopped right in front of me and towered over me. Then, she licked me across the back and head a couple of times to reassure me that all was OK. Grabbing me with her teeth by the back of my neck, she hoisted me high above the earth and trotted with me swinging from her mouth back to where she had been with my brothers and sister. I remember that event because that was the day that I discovered that I wanted to see everything, hear everything, smell everything, taste everything, and touch everything with my paws. In other words, I discovered that I was curious, and I wanted to know all about this huge world.

By the time all of us were eight weeks old, we were eating solid dog kibbles given to us by the kennel keeper. While I often continued to suck mother's milk, I liked feeling my jaw bones make my teeth grind the kibble into smaller pieces to swallow. While I was growing quickly, I was also being taken away from my mother and brothers and sisters by the kennel keeper to visit other dogs. Where I lived, there was a twelve-year-old Pit Bull, who growled deeply at me when I went by. There was also a chihuahua, who barked incessantly. At that time, I made up my mind that I didn't like small barking dogs, and I still don't like them. I never bark back at them; I prefer to walk away. On that trip I met a cat, a creature I thought strange at first, until I assumed a posture of getting ready to give chase. The cat disappeared behind a large bush; I decided that it might be fun to chase cats! See, I didn't know it then, but the kennel keeper was socializing me. She recognized that I was smart and at the head of my litter. Anyway, after my short tour of some of the other residents of the kennel, I was returned to my mother. I pushed my way to her belly for warmth and security and a liquid treat.

On most days, after daylight arrived, mother would be put on a leash and taken out of the kennel for a walk. After a few minutes, she would return and be given a large bowl of food, which she would stand and eat. Then, she would lap up a lot of water from her other bowl. She would lie down and let all of us curl up around her. Sometimes we would suck a teat, while at other times we would eat some of the delicious food put in a couple bowls for us by our kennel keeper. After eating, mother groomed us with her tongue, washing away any dirt and combing our fur just the way she liked it. All of us played with all kinds of small stuffed toys that squeaked when we bit them. I made up my mind that I didn't like squeaky toys and decided that I would chew on them until I found the squeaker and get it out. Sometimes our play was just rolling over each other or hiding behind mother or getting under the rug in our kennel. However, from the time we were three to four weeks old, we played ourselves to sleep.

When we were not running and playing and wagging our tails, we were eating puppy chow. Something instinctively told me to move away from my brothers and sister when I needed to poop. Quickly I learned what the urge to poop felt like, although in those first few days I often did not make it too far away from the rest of the litter! Our kennel keeper made it a point to get mother and my brothers and sister out of the kennel and clean it—sometimes twice a day. She didn't need only to wash away poop, but she had food particles to wash away, too. Any time we ate solid food, we made a mess with kibbles spilled all over the kennel floor.

As we reached the fifth month of our life outside the womb, we ate more puppy chow, drank more water from the water bowl, and sucked less on mother's teats. In fact, it seemed that mother was losing more and more interest in us. She would be gone for long periods of time, but we didn't mind because we ate, played, and slept. When mother would reappear or awaken us, we would greet her with noisy grunts and happy squeaks. There were times when all of us would run to mother after she sat down and push our noses onto a teat, but she would move and shake us lose. She knew that it was best for us to eat solid food, even though we loved to snuggle against her and, while drinking her warm milk, breathe in her smell. Gradually, all of us discovered that there was less and less milk for us to suck. What we were discovering is that mother was just about finished doing her part to raise us.

One day while mother was gone, a person we had never seen before came to our kennel. He picked up each one of us, looking carefully at our eyes and ears and forcing open our mouths. Then, he took a needle and inserted it into the scruff of our necks. It didn't hurt. I overheard that person talking to our kennel keeper about more vaccinations to come. After that experience, our kennel keeper began to take us two at a time to his home. Mother didn't seem to mind that we were gone. In her house, she played with us and talked to us, even though we didn't understand a lot of what she said. When she brought us back to our kennel, she would whistle to let the others and mother know that we were being brought back. Everyone got a turn doing this, except mother, of course, as she already knew what the inside of human houses looked like.

As all of these activities continued, the days went by quickly. Before we knew it, we were five weeks old, no longer yearning for our mother's milk, but enjoying small meals of solid food throughout the day. Mother was still around, using her nose to push us to the bowls of food or to grab us and bring us back to where she wanted us to stay. Mother got upset with us when we bit each other too hard. She would notice that I had bit the ear of one of my brothers, and she would scold me. "It is OK to play and nip each other," I remember her saying, "but biting is reserved for extraordinary occasions. This was a difficult lesson for us to learn, because we forgot it almost as fast as mother taught it. Taking her big front paw, she would swipe it across the puppy who was biting his or her sibling. The guilty puppy would go rolling over and over in the hope that he or she would get the message!

By the time we turned six weeks old, we were still growing, but slowly. The veterinarian, who had examined us before, came back and examined all of us once again. Our kennel keeper began to put puppy pads in our kennel. When one of us began to pee, she would pick us up and put us on the pad. It didn't take long for me to figure out this part of the process. If I felt the urge to pee, I walked over to the pad, and did my business upon it. If I felt the need to poop, I walked over to the pad and left a deposit upon it. After I saw the kennel keeper pick up the pee and poop filled pad and replace it with a clean one, I saw the wisdom in this process. I also learned that outside the kennel on the ground was like finding a pad. I preferred small clumps of grass upon which to pee and poop. With all the training going on, the seventh week of my life went by in a flash. Here I was eating solid food with my brothers and sister. Here I was heading to the pad when I felt the need to pee and poop. While mother checked on us from time to time, it seemed that we saw less and less of her. However, I knew when she was in the area or coming to check on us, because I could smell her from far away.

2

THE EXPLORER

AFTER SPENDING TWO MONTHS with my brothers and sister in the kennel with our mother, all of us were growing and developing our own personalities. We had gone from being sightless and stumbling all over each other to being able to see and explore the world around us with some independence. Our mother disappeared one day and did not return to check on us. As we growled among ourselves in play and jumped for joy, we presumed that she was setting us free to be our own dog, now that we could feed ourselves from our bowls and drink water from our trough. We were putting on weight and growing adult fur, while still being soft and cuddly puppies.

One day the kennel keeper picked up all of us, put us in a cloth box with two screens for windows and took us to a pet store. While we could see very little through the screens, we heard other puppies yelping and crying before we were placed in a fenced-in open area. While we explored this new place with its straw smells, faces of people we had never seen before looked down on us. Often, someone would pick up one of us, turn us over to see if we were male or female, then examine us from nose to tail. Discussions among people were about color. All my brothers and sister were black and white. Some had more black than white, and others had more white than black. The design of black and white on each puppy is what attracted the people to us. Later I learned that the puppy people liked was liked because he or she somehow or other conformed to their expectations of how a dog was supposed to look.

While a few people picked up me, my brindle fur was often described as brown, and brown with streaks of dark cream and highlights of red— although pronounced beautiful—was not what people presupposed the color a dog should be. Therefore, while my brothers began to disappear one by one, and my sister didn't come back after a little girl took her, I was left when the day was done. Because we were not pure breeds, our kennel keeper didn't get as much money from selling us as she would have gotten if our parents had been of the same breed. Nevertheless, in the pet store she sold us—my brothers and sister—on the same day for a cheap rate. She picked up me and put me in the fabric carrier with the two windows and brought me back to the kennel. After being with four brothers and a sister for two months, I was now alone. After she took me out of the box and put me in my kennel, I looked all around the perimeter and smelled ever corner in the hope of discovering a brother or my sister there. But no one was there except me. I broke down and cried. While I nibbled on the bowl of food the kennel keeper brought me, I was not hungry. It was at that moment that I experienced what loneliness is. After getting a drink of water, I lay down on the small rug in the corner, curled into a ball, and cried myself to sleep. If you had looked into my large kennel room, you would have seen a brindle ball of fur with streaks of red that was hidden in the darkness.

The next day, the kennel keeper repeated the previous day's process. She put me in the fabric box with the two windows and took me back to the store where I had been the day before. I was expecting to find my brothers and sister there, but when she put me in the fenced-in area, all I could find were smells of fresh straw. My brothers and sister were gone. But before I could spend too much time dwelling on my loss, a newly-married couple entered the store and came directly over to the place where I was. They were happy, and that made me happy, too. The man reached down into my lonely space and, with his hand wrapped around and under my belly, lifted me up and brought me to his face. In a second, his wife's hand was touching me on my back. I liked their smells. And as I listened to them talk to each other, I heard the words "pretty" and "beautiful." And before I knew it, I was in their car and on the way to my new home. I was eight weeks old, weaned, and ready for my next adventure.

After about a twenty-minute trip in the SUV, we arrived at my new home. Robert and Susan, the names of my new people, parked the car in the garage and took me into their house and placed me on the kitchen floor. Before they could stop me, I ran to the wall and began to smell everything along it. The tile floor was cool on my paws, but changed to carpet as I turned the corner. It had been a few hours since I had peed, and my bladder was full. So, while squatting on the soft, sweet-smelling carpet, I peed. Robert picked me up, and I continued to pee, while he took me out the back door and placed me on the lawn. By the time he got me there, of course, I was finished. Susan had followed him with a mop. He turned and said to her, "She needs to be potty trained." Of course, I had no idea what that meant. At home, I had straw or grass in which to pee and poop.

After bringing me back into the house, Susan scooted me toward a small bowl of food she had prepared and set on the floor. I smelled it and began to eat some of it. It was chicken and some vegetables. I was hungry, so I stuck out my little tongue, got some of its small kibbles in my mouth, chewed a little, swallowed and repeated the process until I had eaten all that was in the bowl. Then, I noticed another bowl near the now empty food bowl. So, I scooted over to it, smelled it, determined that it was water, and lapped up some of it. After eating this big meal, I was tired. So, I returned to the carpeted area, balled up, and fell asleep.

When I awoke, I saw a puppy pad on newspapers in the kitchen just on the other side of the boundary of the carpet. I had seen one of those before when the kennel keeper had put me on it to pee and poop. I felt like I needed to poop, so I moved over to the puppy pad and did so. Robert and Susan were not around; I don't know where they were at that moment. However, within a few seconds they were present praising me, petting me, and cuddling me for having used the puppy pad. Of course, at that time they did not know how smart I was. It usually took only one time showing me what to do for me to get it. I had the puppy pad use down. After they cleaned up my poop, they put down a fresh puppy pad and I went directly over to it and peed on it! While they were not as excited as they were the first time I used it, they realized that I knew what it was for.

While Susan picked up me and put me on her lap, she and Robert began to discuss what name they would give me. All I had ever been called was "Brown Puppy" or "Brindle Puppy." Robert suggested they name be "Brownie," but Susan didn't like that. Then he said, "We should call her 'Snoopy,' because she is always walking around and smelling everything." Finally, Susan said, "I want to name her 'Shelby.'" Robert said, "I have never heard that name before." Susan replied, "My great-grandmother had a brindle dog who was named Shelby. And I want her to have that name." Robert agreed, and from that day on I was known as Shelby. I would learn later that the name comes from two Old Norse words: *selja* (meaning *willow*) and *byr* (meaning *estate*). Thus, Shelby means a *willow estate* or an *estate of willows*. Because willow trees are graceful and elegant, the hope was that the person—in my case, the dog—would be graceful and elegant. I liked my name because I liked its sound from the lips of Robert and Susan. It was pretty, and it described me as graceful and elegant. After Robert and Susan called me Shelby a few times, I was able to recognize it and respond to it by finding or coming to whichever one of them called me.

The first night I stayed in Robert and Susan's house they put me in a fabric box with one window. I had a small blanket upon which to sleep, but they didn't allow for me to be able to get out and use the puppy pad during the night. So, when I had to pee, I went to the corner and did so. Also, I was very much alone in that box. Until two nights before, I had curled up with five other puppies beside me and sometimes on top of me. I could smell each of them, hear their hearts beating, and feel them move around. I didn't like being alone in the box, and I thought that peeing in its corner might enlighten Robert and Susan, who had become my new owners. Needless to say, they were not pleased with the wet box the next morning when they came to see about me. So, Robert took me outside and put me on the grass, where I peed again. He brought me back into the house and told Susan, "I think she can stay out of the box and use the puppy pad. We can try that and see how it works." Susan agreed. It wasn't long before Robert left the house, then Susan went away, leaving me alone to explore.

And explore is what I did. I made my way from my food and water bowls in the kitchen to the carpeted living room area. I smelled my way along the wall to behind the sofa. I just fit between the sofa and the wall and sneezed often from the dust back there. I sniffed my way under the coffee table and around the fireplace. Then, I found an open door and went inside the master bedroom. There were lots of things on the floor to smell and areas to explore. I got to the bathroom and peeked inside. While I walked around a lot of fixtures that smelled like Robert and Susan, I couldn't raise myself high enough to see what was inside of them. So, I continued to explore the bedroom. While under the bed, I found a slipper, and believe me or not it tasted good. So, I lay there under the bed for a while and chewed on Robert's slipper. It felt good to sink my teeth into something other than puppy kibble. After getting bored with the slipper, I slipped out into the hall and entered another room with lots of cardboard boxes. As I walked among them, sniffing their contents and wagging my little tail, I found one that was open and tilted on its side. With little effort I was able to enter it. And to my surprise, I discovered it held a small bag of my puppy food. While smelling the bag, I pushed it over with my nose, and lots of kibbles fell all over the floor. I began to eat a few, and they tasted much better on the floor than they did in a bowl! I ate a few more and more and more. And when I was very full, I fell asleep right there on the floor with kibble all around me. And I slept for a long time. When I awoke, I needed to poop. So, I headed to the puppy pad, but I couldn't make it. While traversing the carpet, the urge overtook me, and I pooped right where I was. As soon as I was finished and felt some relief, I knew Robert and Susan would not be pleased when they got home that evening. After this, I hid behind the sofa because I was ashamed of what I had done.

I heard the garage door go up later that day, and I heard Susan walk into the house. She called, "Shelby," but I did not respond. Then, as she walked through the kitchen, her nose twitched; she smelled my poop on the carpet before she saw it. However, like me she followed her nose to the spot, and yelled, "Shelby." I stayed where I was. She yelled my name again, and again I stayed where I was. Instead of looking for me, she went to work cleaning the mess I had left on the carpet. She put on rubber gloves and came into the living room with a bucket of warm, soapy water. Using paper towels, she scooped up my poop and put it into a plastic bag she had brought with her. Then, using a rag, she scrubbed the carpet with the soapy water in the bucket. Several times she wetted the rag, cleaned the carpet, and rinsed the rag. It took her three attempts, but she got the poop stain out of the carpet, and when the stain disappeared, so did the poop smell. After emptying the bucket and placing it and the rag in the garage, she reentered the house and began to look for me. She called, "Shelby, Shelby." I stuck my head out from behind the sofa. With head lowered I gradually crawled out to where she had knelt down. I was hoping to be picked up and cuddled. Susan picked me up and abruptly placed me near the spot where my poop had been. Then, she raised her hand and slapped me across the back, sending me rolling across the floor. She came and got me and brought be back to the spot on the carpet and slapped me again, sending me rolling again. Then, with the sternest voice, she said, "Don't ever do that again!" Then, she walked away, leaving me all alone in my shame. I cried while scooting back behind the sofa, where I curled up and lay down. I stayed there until Robert came home.

When I heard his voice in the kitchen, I emerged from hiding to see him talking to Susan. I knew she was telling him about my mishap on the carpet. He said, "Shelby is just a puppy; we have to expect such things." Then, he went to the bedroom to change out of his work clothes and put on comfort clothes. When he looked under the bed to get his slippers, he found the one I had chewed on. With the slipper in hand he rushed into the living room, where I was lying on the carpet. Immediately, I noticed that his face was redder than usual. He walked over to me and took the slipper and hit me across the back with it. I was stunned, but only for a second. He took his foot and scooted it under me and tossed me in the air. I rolled and rolled over the carpet. Then, he came after me again with the slipper, slapping me with it again before throwing it down and yelling, "If you ever do that again I'll kill you!" Instinctively, I knew I was in trouble. So, I managed to get up and scurry back behind the sofa, where I cried myself to sleep.

Later that evening, Susan put some food in my bowl and called me to come and eat it. Shivering, I slipped out of my hiding place and to my bowl. I ate my food, after which Susan took me to the backyard, where I walked around a little before peeing and pooping. When we came in, she put an old towel in my fabric box and put me in the box on top of the towel and zipped it closed. Then, she and Robert went to bed. I was left in the kitchen in a box. At some time during the night, I needed to pee and poop again, but there was nowhere to go except in the corner of my box. While falling back to sleep, I accidentally got some of the poop on me. I could smell it, but there was nothing I could do about it. The next morning, Susan was up first. She unzipped the box and saw that I had poop on my fur and became furious. She put on rubber gloves and lifted me out of the box and took me to the back yard where she threw me onto the grass. I lay there for a long time after Susan went back into the house. I guess she told Robert what

I did, because he came to the back yard and unwound the garden hose. Then, within a few feet of me he turned it on and began to spray me with it. Because I weighed only about twenty pounds, he sprayed me across the yard rolling me over and over as he did so. "That will teach you to poop in your box," he said. I was all wet, but it wasn't cold. I was all alone on the grass. I had no food or water, when I heard both cars leave the garage. I stayed there all day.

While I explored the yard, I dried off. I found all kinds of interesting smells along the fence that enclosed the backyard. I tried to catch a few squirrels, but they ran up the tree trunks to branches high above me. A rabbit appeared in the flower garden wiggling its nose as it munched on leaves of grass. I approached the rabbit to smell it, but he hopped off and disappeared in a hole under the storage shed. After a while I began to get hungry. My little tummy growled, and I wished that I had a bowl of water. I found a cool spot in the shade by the shed, and I attempted to dig a hole in which to lie. I was able to move some soil, but got my paws all muddy and my belly all dirty. Finally, Susan came home and remembered to check on me. After she saw the hole I had dug and how dirty I was, she went back into the house and left me outside by myself. It began to rain, and the rain was cold. While the heavenly water was washing the dirt off of me, I began to shiver. I tried to find shelter near the back door, but the rain still blew on me. Finally, Robert came home, and Susan sent him to check on me. By now the rain shower had stopped, but I was still shivering. As he had done earlier, he took the hose and sprayed whatever dirt was still clinging to me. The spray was so forceful that it knocked me over and rolled me over. Robert just laughed and laughed. Then, he did pick up my very wet and dripping self, took me into the house, and wrapped me in a towel to dry me. Once that was finished, he put me on the floor near my food and water bowls. Susan had put food and water out. I was famished. So, I went to the food bowl and ate kibble after kibble before going to the water bowl and lapping up lots of the refreshing liquid.

These experiences repeated themselves often. I longed to be held and petted. I wanted to snuggle with Robert and Susan, but all they said to me was, "Bad dog!" I couldn't do anything that would make them happy. I had been with them for a week which felt like a month. I was not feeling a part of this family. I was scared, as could be determined by the fact that when they let me inside, I spent most of my time behind the sofa. Every day both of them left the house, usually leaving me outside. I spent the night in my box, which I started to think about as a cage, trying to hold on until the morning when one of them took me to the backyard to pee and poop. Sometimes, they fed me and put fresh water in my bowl; sometimes they forgot to feed me, and I drank whatever water was still in my bowl. Left outside when it rained, I tried to find a place for shelter. When relatives or friends of Robert and Susan came to the house, I was introduced to them as Shelby. Then, I was either fed and put into my cage or put outside. I spent many nights shivering and afraid in the darkness, but, ultimately, I would fall asleep in a ball and awaken when the first light of dawn had appeared.

By the time I was three months old, I had grown a lot and learned how to control my bladder and poop muscle. One day Robert took me to a veterinarian I had never met before and had me checked over. I also got a shot in the scruff of my neck and other medications that were to be given to me at set times. The vet talked to me softly and told me how pretty I was, but he didn't know about the slapping, kicking, or hose-spraying that Robert and Susan continued to use to try to make me do what they wanted. I wanted to spend the day inside the house; I didn't like the humid, hot weather. So, I continued to dig the hole by the storage shed, which got me sprayed more. I didn't like being kicked, but it happened so fast that I did not have time to run away. Likewise, I didn't like being slapped, but I didn't understand why chewing on a shoe, a pillow, or a table leg was so bad! Yes, I was smart enough to know better, but I was bored and in desperate need of stimulation. I figured that Robert and Susan only wanted the idea of a dog; they didn't want a real dog. Or, they wanted a dumb dog, but they got a smart dog.

3

ADULT PUPPYHOOD

Robert and Susan were gone all day, and they left me in the backyard. Sometimes they remembered to put out food and water for me, but other times I had to wait until one of them came home in the late afternoon or early evening. There were a few times when it was late evening when someone finally remembered that I was still outside in the backyard. On weekends, they might be gone from Friday to Sunday. The only people I knew were Robert and Susan. Robert had tried to play with me by tossing a ball, but I saw no sense in running after a ball. He was upset that I wouldn't play and kicked me. Susan kept her distance from me, often putting me in my crate when I was in the house. I presumed that she didn't want to have to clean poop off the carpet! When someone I didn't know showed up, I wasn't sure how to act. Should I bark? Should I go and smell him or her? Should I seek attention? I was full of fear that I would do the wrong thing and get slapped or kicked away. I knew that Robert did not like the den (hole) I was fashioning in the backyard by the storage shed, but he had decided to stop filling it in. All he said to me was, "Bad dog!" over and over again. The next opportunity I got, I removed the soil he had placed in it and continued enlarging it where I had left off the previous time digging. I was sure that I would get kicked if he ever caught me near it.

Not only was I growing bigger, but I was getting smarter. I had learned to stay behind the sofa when I was in the house, and to come out only to eat or to get a drink of water. When I was left outside, I had learned where to find a cool space in the hole I had expanded under the storage shed, where to get out of the rain when it fell, and to stay away from the coiled hose attached to the outdoor spicket. I noticed that my baby teeth were falling out and adult teeth were beginning to fill my mouth. I longed for things to chew on. In the house, I had a few stuffed toys that I carried behind the sofa. I would either sit or lie down with them and chew and chew. Outside, sticks from the overhead trees fell on the lawn regularly. Unless it was too big for me to carry, I'd pick up a stick and carry it to my den and spend some of the day chewing on wood. Something else I learned to love to do was to watch cars passing on the street in my neighborhood. At one spot along the fence, I could see the street. I'd sit there watching cars and trucks go by intermittently, and on dark, cloudy days I would become mesmerized by their headlights.

All I had ever had on me was a small collar around my neck. While it was snug, it was not tight. Plus, it had a tag attached to it that had my name engraved on it along with Robert's telephone number. One day when I was almost six months old, Robert came to the back yard carrying a contraption with lots of cloth strips. He called, "Shelby!" When I didn't appear immediately, he shouted, "Shelby!" Sheepishly, I came forward and stood before him. He knelt down in front of me, making me leery that he was about to do something to me. He told me, "Sit!" but I didn't know what that meant. So, he pushed me down onto my back legs and said, "Sit!" OK, I thought, I get it. Then, he took the cloth strips, which I now could see were attached to each other and slipped the round one over my head. Then, he raised my right foot and passed it through a cloth strip, then my left foot through a cloth strip. At the back of my head, I felt him pull the strips around my front legs taught and tighten them in place. I didn't know what was happening, until Susan came to the backyard and said, "So that is how the harness fits." Robert said, "Yes. Now all I have to do is attach the leash, and we'll take Shelby for a walk." Taking a longer piece of cloth, I felt him open a buckle and place it around the ring on my harness. Then, he jerked the leash, pulling me up, and he and Susan headed for the back gate. Since I had never been in a harness before, I didn't know that it was to keep me from wandering away while we attempted to walk together.

The harness has a mesh oblong patch that pressed against my breast. When Robert pulled the leash, the mesh would either jerk me in the direction he wanted to go or it would stop me from proceeding farther in the direction my nose wanted to take me. It was a good thing that they only went two blocks down the street. I doubt that I could have endured much more jerking and pulling. I figured out that they wanted me to walk either in front of them or beside them. I figured out that they wanted me to stay on the sidewalk even though my nose was leading me to the nearest clump of grass or bush or tree trunk. Whenever I headed toward one of those objects, I got pulled back to the concrete path. After two blocks, I think I had it down, but they turned around and walked home quicker than my legs could carry me. So, I was dragged part of the way home. I knew how this was supposed to work; I just needed to get bigger, stronger, and faster. This was my first step outside my house and yard, and from the little I got to smell and see, I determined that I wanted to smell and see a lot more.

By the time I turned six months old on October 7, 2012, I was becoming a handsome dog, although few people ever saw me besides Robert and Susan. While I conformed to their expectations of always peeing and pooping outside, staying behind the sofa except to eat my two meals a day and to get a drink of water from time to time, and either stretching out under the storage shed or sitting by the fence and watching the cars pass, I led a very boring life. When they took me for a walk, I tried to smell things, but they were not interested in me. They wanted to walk and to walk fast. So, I gave up trying to smell things and just kept up the pace, unless I needed to pee or poop. After I pooped, I noticed that one of them would pull a plastic bag out of his or her pocket and with the bag on his or her hand bend over and pick up the poop. Then, turning the bag outside-in so the poop was enclosed in it, he or she would twist its top and tie a knot in it. One of them would carry the poop bag through the rest of the walk—or until we came to trash can into which it was deposited—and bring it home and put it in our trash cart.

A few days after my six-month birthday, I was taken to the veterinarian. I had heard Robert and Susan talking about "spaying Shelby," but I had no idea what that meant. While I had only been in a vet's office a couple of times, I hated the cramped examination room. I hated the smells. I knew other dogs and cats had been in there. The bench was hard to sit on. I weighed forty-one pounds. I had not yet had my first heat, which I heard the vet tell Robert was the perfect time for me to be spayed. Of course, I did not know what that meant. The vet took my leash and led me out of the examination room, even though I planted all four feet and didn't want to move, to the operating room. There, an assistant drew a vial of blood from my neck and took it to the laboratory in another room. She returned shortly to tell the vet, "Everything is normal." I was getting very nervous, so the vet injected a sedative to quiet me. I became very drowsy, although I did not fall asleep. I remember the vet's assistant cutting away a small section of the fur on my right paw, swabbing it with alcohol, and inserting an intravenous catheter, which was to supply me with a saline solution. Then, the vet placed general anesthesia in the line, and I fell asleep for a very long time.

When I awakened, I felt pain in my belly. I was very groggy from the anesthesia, so I could not move. There was also a cone around my head so I could not see or lick the area on my body from where the pain was coming. Later, I learned what spay meant. The veterinarian had made an incision in my abdomen below my belly button and, using an instrument called a spay hook, found my uterus and brought it out of the incision. Once he located my ovaries, he clamped them and sutured them before removing them with a scalpel. After he was sure that there was no bleeding, he replaced the uterus in my abdomen. Then, with three layers of sutures he closed the opening in my abdomen and placed a bandage over the wound. He gave me an injection of pain medication. That is why when I awoke in recovery, I was so groggy. When she saw that I was awake, the vet's assistance took me to a small kennel in which she placed me on a blanket. The vet told Robert that it was a good idea if I spent the night there. He could come and get me in the morning, if all was well. That evening, I was given a little food, which I devoured, and some water to drink. In the food was some pain medication, which I know I tasted, but I felt so bad and was so hungry that I just swallowed it.

The next day both Robert and Susan came to get me. Robert carried me to the car and lay me on a blanket in the back seat, and Susan covered me with a portion of the blanket. They took me home and out of the car and placed me on a pallet made of old blankets that Susan had prepared for me on the kitchen floor. They gave me more pain medication and some food and water. The cone kept me from seeing the incision, upon which Susan placed a fresh bandage every day. After a while, I was able to get up, but it was very difficult to walk with the cone around my head and the pain medication, which made me very groggy. However, I did manage to take a few steps to the puppy pad that Robert had placed near my pallet in order to pee and poop. As the days went by, the pain lessened. When Robert and Susan were gone, they put me in the fabric box to keep me from too much activity. I heard Susan tell Robert, "She needs to stay still so she doesn't pull open the incision." By two weeks, I was feeling like my old self. It hurt a little when Robert and Susan let me go outside to walk a little, to pee, and to poop, but it was not like the pain of the first two or three days following the surgery. The cone was taken off my head and I was able to see where the incision, which had now healed, had been made in my belly.

While lying in the sun in the yard three weekends after my surgery, I began to reflect on the consequences of the spaying. When Robert and Susan had taken me for a walk and we met someone else walking a male dog, that dog always smelled my butt. A few times he wanted to jump on my back, but his owner always pulled him away. Now I realized that he was hoping I was in heat and he wanted to inseminate me in order to reproduce. Reproduction for me was now out of the question, since my ovaries had been removed. I would not be able to contribute my set of DNA to any puppies. That meant that there would be no brindle puppy being born from my womb, that no puppies would every nurse at my nipples, that no puppies would ever depend upon me for care. While the kicking and hose-spraying had stopped during my recuperation and I had not hidden behind the sofa, now I felt more alone than ever.

While I enjoyed my time in the house during recuperation, after my wound was healed, I was back to staying in the backyard. I was sent there in the morning after breakfast before Robert and Susan left to go to work, and I stayed there until they came home in late afternoon or early evening. The backyard was where I peed and pooped as far away from the house and as close to the fence as possible. Before he mowed, Robert had to look around and pick up the poop so he wouldn't step in it. One Saturday, however, he missed a pile and stepped in it while mowing. It made him very upset. He grabbed a stick that had fallen out of the big tree in the backyard and came toward me. I thought he was coming to pet me or give me a command, but instead he took the stick and beat me three times on the back with it. I cried and barked at the same time. I cried because it hurt and left whelps on my skin, and I barked because I wanted to attack him and bite him. He broke the stick on my back, scraped his shoe in the grass to remove my poop from it, and went back to the mower to continue cutting the grass.

A few days later, he came to the storage shed and, for some reason, looked at the back, where he noticed the hole I had dug at the back of the shed and partially under it. That is where I spent most of the day because the dirt was cool in the summer and warm in the winter. When it rained and lightning and thundered, I could scoot under the shed for protection; it gave me a little security as I shivered in fear of the thunder claps and the flashes of lightning. Robert was not aware of how large the hole had become. So, he yelled, "Shelby! Shelby! Get over here right now!" Dutifully, I slowly walked to where he was standing. I did not notice that he had a stick in his hand, with which he struck me once, twice, and the stick broke. "I want this digging to stop," he shouted. "Do you understand?" I lay on the ground and lowered my head in shame, expecting to get struck again, but he walked away to attend to whatever he was doing.

Since I was prohibited from digging a hole, which Robert had filled in with soil and planted grass seed, I began to study the backyard fence. It was chain-linked about six feet high with a gate that opened onto the side of the house and, hence, to the street. After studying the gate for a while one day, I attempted to squeeze through an area where it met the fence post for latching. I had already tried to raise the latch with my nose, but it was too tight. After studying it for a while, I decided to dig a hole under it, because it was a little bit higher than the rest of the fence that sat on the ground. I discovered that the soil was soft and easy to remove. So, with all four paws—two in front disturbing the soil and two in back whisking it away—I began excavating a passageway under the gate. Within a few hours of hard work I was able to slither under the gate through the tunnel I had excavated and found myself on the other side of the fence. While I had been there before on a leash with Robert and Susan, I had never been there alone before. So, I began to smell everything—clumps of grass, flowers in the garden that had been created there, rocks, and more. I stopped to pee on everything. I was in no hurry; I took my time to see what was there.

Suddenly, I saw a black and gray cat, and I leaped at the chance to chase it. It ran next door to the neighbor's porch, where I cornered it, barking, barking, and barking at it. The neighbor lady opened the door to see what was going on and found me sitting in front of the cat in the corner. She knew I belonged next door. So, she grabbed my collar and led me across her yard and back to the gate, where she saw how I had escaped. She opened the gate and put me in my backyard, and, taking her foot, scraped the dirt back into the hole I had dug under the gate. Then, taking a few stones from the flower garden, placed them on top of the dirt, effectively keeping me from digging the tunnel again.

After Susan got home that afternoon, she received a call from the neighbor lady, who explained what had happened. Susan emerged from the back door in a furry, walked to the gate, examined the mess, and yelled, "Shelby! Shelby! Get over here right now!" I knew I was in trouble, but I obeyed, walking slowly to where Susan was standing by the gate. "Did you do this?" she asked me. I lowered my head as an admission of guilt. "I thought we told you to stop digging holes! Wait here." Going into the storage shed, she got a shovel. I thought she was going to fix the tunnel I had created. Instead, she took the handle and wacked me across the back. I yelped in pain. I tried to move away, but she hit me again, and I just fell to the ground. She went to the gate and began to remove the stones and place them where they belonged and shovel all the dirt into the hole and stomp it down.

After she went back into the house, I managed to walk to the area behind the storage shed. I lay down and cried because my back hurt from the beating I had received. For a few moments my spirit was crushed. All I wanted to do was to escape. However, when Robert got home and Susan narrated the story of what happened, he came to the gate and examined the scene of the crime. I emerged from my hiding place to see what he was doing. He picked up the hose and sprayed me with it over and over and over again, laughing all the while. "That will teach you to tunnel under the gate," he said.

Well, it only made me more determined to get out of that yard. The next day, I continued my study of the gate. Instead of tunneling under it, I decided I might be able to push against it hard enough to force its latch open. It was easier than tunneling! I pushed my nose into the opening, then squeezed my head through—even though it hurt my ears. With my back legs pushing and my front legs pulling, I used my shoulders and forced the latch to turn lose. The gate swung open. After a year of life, I was now free, but I had nowhere to go! If I left here, I would be a stray dog, who would be caught by the dog catcher, stopped by a neighbor, or hit by a car when trying to cross the street. While I might find some water in a ditch or creek, who would feed a stray dog? After exploring the neighborhood, I came home, went through the open gate, and hid behind the storage shed. When Robert got home and saw the open gate, he beat me again, closed the gate, put a lock on the latch, and said, "Tomorrow, you will be tied to the tree."

And that is exactly what happened. Around the tree he placed a large length of chain. One end had a spring-latch that, once wrapped around the tree's trunk, was closed on a link on the chain. The other end also had a spring-latch, which was attached to the ring on my collar. After putting me in the backyard that morning, Robert grabbed me by the collar and pulled me to the chain, which he attached to me. My range of motion was limited to about six feet. The chain was too short for me to hide behind the storage shed. All I could do was lie on the grass and move periodically either into the sun or into the shade. I walked as far away as I could get to pee and poop throughout the day, trying to keep an area clean for me to rest in. I hated being tied, but I had a plan. The next morning after I was affixed to the chain and Robert left, I turned around with my head toward the tree and I began to take steps back. As the chain got tighter and tighter, I lowered my head a little and, taking several small steps backward, felt the collar around my neck begin to slip over my head. With a few wiggles, the collar came off, and I was free! While the gate was locked, and the tunnel under it had been covered with weighty pavers that I could not move with my paws, I was able to explore the yard and spend time behind the storage shed. When she came home, Susan found me unattached. "How did you get that collar off?" she asked. "I don't know what we are going to do with you." Coming forward to greet her, I got a kick in the side. When Robert got home and Susan told him what I did, he was upset, but for some unknown reason did not beat me.

The next day they left me in the house while they went to work. I loved staying in the house because it was cool in the summer and warm in the winter. After stretching out in the sun coming into the house through a window for a few hours, I got bored. I went to Robert and Susan's bedroom and jumped onto their bed, which was soft and cozy. So, I took the opportunity to roll around on it. I rolled from side to side, and I lay on my back with all four feet in the air for a while. I rolled over and over, wiggling with my head and hips. I had so much fun playing that I didn't notice how wrinkled I left the quilt when I jumped off the bed. Passing through the living room to my water bowl in the kitchen, I spotted the sofa, behind which I hid a lot. I jumped on the sofa and some of the many pillows fell onto the floor. Grabbing one pillow with my teeth, I tugged it over to an open area and played with it on the carpet. With my legs I'd roll it underneath of me and throw it around, getting it, scratching it, and rolling it around again. I noticed an area that was perfect for getting my teeth into. As I began to pull on the lose threads there, the opening got larger and larger until I was able to get small pieces of the foam out of the pillow. Dutifully, I placed bite after bite of the pillow stuffing on either side of me as I lay spread eagle on the carpet. I knew not to eat it, but I had much fun pulling it out of the pillow!

By the middle of the afternoon, after napping in the pillow stuffing, I was hungry. Robert and Susan had not left any food in my bowl, but I knew where it was kept on the lower shelf in the kitchen. The shelf was at my height, so it was easy for me to grab the bag of kibble with my mouth and pull it onto the floor, where enough spilled out for my lunch. As I licked up kibbles, I spotted the box of Milk Bone treats. I pushed it with my nose, and it fell to the floor unleashing treat after treat of seven delicious flavors. Going to each bone, I licked it to taste it, then began to crunch it in my mouth. I was in dog heaven, eating bone after bone after bone! After a while, however, I began not to feel so good. I got up and walked back into the living room, and before I knew it, I was regurgitating pieces of Milk Bones on the carpet. I knew I was in trouble, so I went to hide behind the sofa in the hope that no one would notice.

But, of course, as soon as she came into the house, Susan did notice. "Oh, no!" she yelled when she first entered the kitchen and saw kibbles and bones strewn over the floor. Then, using words I had never heard before, she entered the living room and saw my vomit on the carpet. I did not come out of hiding. Then, she stopped to pick up what was left of the pillow I had opened, and now she was crying. She picked up the other pillows that belonged on the sofa. Going to the bedroom, she could tell that I had been on the bed from the wrinkles in the quilt. Walking back into the living room, she shouted, "Where are you?" Then, changing her tone of voice, she called me softly, "Shelby! Shelby! Come here, girl." I responded by emerging from my hiding place. The tone of voice changed immediately. "You damn dog," she said. "I am getting rid of you as soon as I can." I whimpered and lay down." Susan walked away.

When Robert came home later that day, she told him about everything I did. He called me over and over again, but I would not leave my safe place behind the sofa. That night I was given no food and put in the backyard. Of course, it thundered, there was lightning, and it rained, and I shivered from both being wet and afraid. Ultimately, Robert talked Susan into keeping me. He told her, "I'll try to teach Shelby how to behave. We'll enroll her in obedience school." Reluctantly, Susan agreed to give that a try.

4

SHELTERS

ROBERT TOOK ME TO obedience school. A man told Robert what to say and do in order to discipline me. I learned the meaning of commands, like "Sit," and "Stop," but I was determined not to lose my free spiritedness. Because I was smart, I was able to understand and do whatever I was told. I did it in the hope of being treated with respect. However, at home, Robert and Susan had decided that they would torture me into submission. Thus, I received more beatings with sticks from the yard, with a broom handle, a shovel handle, a mop handle, and whatever else might be available to whack me. Instead of being petted, I got slapped, sometimes not even knowing why. I got kicked for no reason. I got sprayed with the hose. I got left outside in the rain with the thunder and the lightning. Yes, they fed me when they thought of it, and they usually left water for me to drink in a bowl. Yes, they took me to the veterinarian at least once a year to get my vaccinations. Yes, they took me on walks and jerked the leash to pull me back into place when I wanted to explore a tree truck or a clump of grass or something else.

I did not change my behavior. I dug holes in the yard. I got the collar off my neck repeatedly. I even learned how to climb the chain-linked fence. In the house, when left alone, I played on the bed, jumped on the sofa, spilled food onto the floor, and more. I'd pay for all this with beatings, slappings, kickings, etc. This went on for three more years. One day, after I had knocked the pillows off the sofa and Susan came home, she slapped me very hard. And I responded by biting her hand. I was tired of being beaten. I didn't do any damage, but I did cause a little blood to appear on the back of the hand I had sunk my teeth into. She grabbed my collar, drug me through the house to the backdoor, opened it, and pulled me into the backyard. I hurried to my hiding place behind the storage shed. I knew I would be in more trouble when Robert got home and she told him what I had done. And so it happened. Robert came to the backyard. He called me, "Shelby! Shelby! Come here." I went. "We're done with you," is all he said before going back into the house to be with Susan. I was left all alone in the yard.

What I discovered is that Robert and Susan had decided to move to another city because Robert got a better job elsewhere. In the fourth year of my life, they decided not to take me with them because I had bitten Susan. One day Robert took me to the local pet shelter, a place I had never been to before. As he pulled me out of the car, I could hear dogs barking and barking. Quickly, he led me into the building, and he handed me over to a person I had never seen before. She took the leash and other things in a box that Robert gave her, things that were associated with me, and guided me to a kennel with a concrete floor with a drain in the middle, and a six-foot-high fence around it, a rug in the corner, and a bowl with water in another corner. Robert abandoned me there. I never saw him or Susan again. After a few hours I was taken out of the kennel, examined by a vet, led back to my cell, given some food, and left there for the night. All the while I heard dogs barking all around me and echoing off the tile walls and concrete floors of the shelter.

I was in the shelter for about six months. All kinds of people would come and look at me. Some would say, "What a beautiful dog Shelby is." They knew my name because it was on a tag attached to my kennel. A few took me out of my kennel, attached a leash to my collar, and took me for a short walk. "How pretty she is," several people said. However, when they asked the shelter representative about me, she explained, "She came here because she bit her owner." And that was all it took for a visitor to find another dog to adopt. After six months in that shelter, and not being adopted, I was placed in a portable kennel, loaded onto a truck, and taken to another shelter far, far away. I was lucky because both shelters focused on finding me a home and not euthanizing me or any dogs in the shelter. So, after being transported to a different shelter, I was given a different kennel, which was very similar to the one in which I had spent six months, in the hope that someone would adopt me. As in the first shelter, many people came by my cell; some even took me out, but all of them put me back when they read my rap sheet. I had a reputation, and no adult wanted me around their children. There were days when I was so rejected that I didn't even raise my head to look at the person speaking to me outside the fence of my kennel. "What a beautiful dog!" quickly echoed away as I remained in my cell for six more months. All of my fifth year of life was spent in a kennel in a shelter until one day a young man named Corbin came to see me.

Corbin was a college student. He wore dark curly blonde hair, a scraggly blonde beard, and spoke gently and kindly to me. He got permission to put me on a leash and take me outside the shelter. He sat on the grass by me and talked to me. Little did he know that I was understanding a lot of what he was saying! After being in shelters for a year, I had lost most hope of ever getting out. I had tried relentlessly, but my calculations always failed when it came to escaping. Plus, I was weak from being cooped in my cell. Corbin came and set me free, except for letting me off the leash, of course. For thirty minutes he talked to me, played with me, patted my head and my back, rubbed my belly, and then took me back to my cell. I remember thinking, "Dare I hope to be taken home?"

A few days passed, and he came back to see me again. I remember him saying, "I read your rap sheet, Shelby, and I can't believe that you bit someone. I think you are so pretty. I'm thinking seriously about taking you home with me, but not today. I live with four other male college students, and I need to talk to them about you." After more petting, belly rubbing, and hugging and kissing me, he brought me back to my cell, detached the leash, and let me walk in. I asked myself, "Is he telling me the truth? Does he really think my brindle coat is pretty? Does he like how my red highlights sparkle in the sunshine?" As I lay on my rug in my kennel, I dared to hope.

Two days later, he was back. He put me on a leash, took me outside, told me, "Sit"—which I did—petted me, talked to me, kissed me, hugged me, told me that I was going home with him. A big smile came upon my face, and for the first time since I was a puppy, I hunkered down, wanting to play. He told me, "I have decided to adopt you. I want a dog, and you are the dog I have chosen." I knew that word "chosen." He picked me! Then, he led me to the desk in the shelter, paid my adoption fee, asked a few questions about me, led me out and to his car, removed the leash from my collar, opened the door, and bade me to get in the back seat. I was so weak that I could barely jump into the car, but I summoned all the strength I had and leaped into the car of my new owner. He drove me to the apartment complex, parked the car, and called me to get out. He put on my leash, and guided me up the steps to his second-floor apartment. I had to take it very slowly leaping from one step to the next. I was so tired and out of shape! I got to the door, Corbin opened it, and inside I found three of the four other guys who lived there. Each of them presented one hand for me to smell, then patted my head, while Corbin opened a bag of dog food and put some in a tin bowl. He placed the bowl on the floor and invited me to come over and eat. Then, he filled another tin bowl of water near it. I was hungry, and I ate freedom food that afternoon, and I drank freedom water. Later, Corbin introduced me to his girlfriend, Danielle, known as Dani.

I loved it in that apartment. I had people around all the time. Corbin took me for a walk every day, and some days others took me for a walk, too. Over the next few weeks, I gained strength in my legs for climbing the steps, and I put on a few pounds that I had lost being in the shelter system for a year. I had been adopted by a whole group of people. Corbin began to take me running with him. That was OK as long as it was cool, but when it was hot, I just wanted to stop for a while. He also took me to a pet store, where I found cow tracheas, which I used to get one out of a box and bring home with me after Corbin paid for it. I would lie on the carpet and crunch and crunch on its long greasy-covered surface, while I held it in my paws. Corbin also took me to a dog park, where, as long as I was good, I could run and play with other dogs. All of that fall I was fed, watered, cared for, petted, belly rubbed, and loved. Several times Corbin took me home with him to visit his parents about an hour away. I had learned the word "ride." That is all that Corbin had to say to me in order to get me to bound down the steps of the apartment and get ready to leap into the back seat of his car. I liked riding in a car. Corbin's parents welcomed me into their home. Because they had doors with handles instead of knobs, I figured out quickly how to jump up, press down on the handle, and let myself out! They owned a dog, with whom I liked to play. I remember taking his favorite toy—a green bone—and putting it in a cloth bag that had some items Corbin and Dani had brought with them. They did not discover that I had stolen the green bone until they got home and discovered it in the bag!

When we went to visit his parents, who lived in the country, Corbin would often set me free from my leash. I loved to go find the cows that his grandfather ran in the pasture and chase them. I also discovered what a lovely scent cow manure had; when I could get away with it, I would roll and roll and roll in it until it was all over me! When I returned to the house, Corbin had to give me a bath to remove the sweet-smelling perfume I had put on! When the cows were elsewhere, I liked chasing the deer that came into the pasture to feed. I crept slowly toward them, and before they could smell me jumped out. They ran and ran, and I ran after them, never catching one. They were much bigger than I. I now weighed about fifty-eight pounds, and they were much heavier than that. It was so much fun to be so free and run through the pasture and woods. Except for the ticks, of course. After being in the woods and pasture, Corbin would sit down beside me and look me over from nose to tail. He would rub me all over. When he found a tick, he would take it off me if it was still crawling; if it had bit me, he would pull it off my skin and kill it. I didn't like the detaching tick procedure, but I knew it was necessary to keep me healthy. Even though he or Dani put anti-tick and flea medicine on me, I always managed to pick up a few ticks when I was running free through the pasture and woods.

All of that fall I was in recuperation mode. I had lots of people around me. I could get attention anytime. There was always someone around to pet me and scratch my belly. I loved to sit next to someone on the sofa in the apartment and, ultimately, lay down near him until I fell into a deep sleep, snoring. I would often be found softly barking or whimpering or moving my legs while I slept. In my dreams, I was remembering all that had been done to me, and I was always running to hide behind the sofa or behind the storage shed. I would awaken and realize that all that was in the past. I had a new owner and the new owner's girlfriend, and they took care of me. They kept me inside, except for walks of course. They took me on rides to places, like Corbin's home, Dani's home, and to visit Corbin's friend, Mark.

The first time I visited Mark, he was very surprised to see me, a dog in his house. I listened as he explained to Corbin that, while he had grown up in the country, dogs were not permitted in the house. As I listened to that discussion, I sat quietly on the rug between his living room and dining room. I remember him asking Corbin, "Is she hungry?" He replied, "I'll feed her after we get home." Corbin and Mark ate dinner, and I stayed on the rug. After a while I got bored, and I jumped in a large wing-backed chair and curled up for a nap, but Mark came immediately and made me get out. "I don't want you on the furniture," he said. See, at the apartment, I was free to sit on the sofa and chairs. I slept on the bed with Corbin and Dani. At Corbin's parents' home, I jumped onto the sofa or ottoman. Mark, however, made it clear that he did not want me on the furniture. Nevertheless, I had to test out this theory to be sure. So, a few minutes later, I jumped onto the chair again, and he quickly made me get out of it. Later in the evening, after dinner and while he and Corbin were in the living room, and Mark was sitting in the chair I had attempted to sleep in, he reached down and petted me. I rolled over on my side, and he rubbed by belly. While I was not pleased about not being able to sit in the chair—or anywhere else I would later learn—he was a nice man. Of course, at that point in time I didn't know that I would be spending a lot more time in Mark's house.

Mark was impressed with me on that first visit. While I was sitting on the rug between the living room and dining room, he came over to me and commanded, "Shake." And I extended my right paw, which he took and shook! Then, he said, "Roll over," and I did. He petted me. I stood up to get a better view of him, and he said, "Sit." And I sat. He said to Corbin, "I think she is a very smart dog!" I remember thinking, "If he only knew how smart I am!" From time to time, Corbin took me with him to Mark's house. The third time I was there, Mark offered me a bone from a box he had bought for me. I was very hungry, so I ate it. He got me another one, and I ate it, too. While he and Corbin were eating, Corbin would often slip me a bite or two of food. While I stayed off the furniture, I found Mark's home to be a pleasant place to be. He had a back yard to which I was taken to pee, lots of rooms to explore, and a basement full of smells. I visited Mark often.

Over Christmas that year, Mark and Corbin traveled, and Dani was responsible for taking care of me. The college guys living in the apartment all left and went home for Christmas; only Dani and I remained. She had to work, so I was alone. She would put me into the big wire kennel before she left the apartment. Even though I had a bowl of water and a rug upon which to sleep, my freedom was taken away when pushed into the kennel. I got bored long before she came home and let me out and took me for a walk. So, one day I spilled the water on the carpet. On another day, I peed on the carpet. She cleaned up both messes, only scolding me for what I did. I hated that kennel, but, because she didn't trust me, she put me in it every time she left. Once Corbin got back a few days after Christmas, being imprisoned in the kennel was a thing of the past. The other residents of the apartment's five bedrooms and two bathrooms came back after Christmas, and everything resumed as it was before. I had company all day. I was taken on walks, petted, belly rubbed, fed, watered, and never once slapped, beaten, kicked, or tied. Almost every week when Corbin went to Mark's house, I went along. Mark purchased good dog food for me, and he put it in a plastic bowl to eat while he and Corbin ate their dinner. After I ate my food, I got a bone or two for dessert. And I stayed off the furniture.

In May, after college classes were finished, Corbin and Dani moved into a studio apartment, and they took me with them. I didn't like the studio apartment as soon as I saw it. It was too small; there was little to explore. There were no other people around; only Corbin and Dani. So, the first time they both left the studio apartment, they put me in my wire kennel. I had decided that I was not going to stay in there for hours and hours of boredom. So, by studying the way it was made, if I turned my head sideways, I was able to stick my nose in between the bars and turn it in order to push them apart. Then, I could grab the cross bars with my mouth and move them back and forth until they broke off. While the black paint tasted awful, it didn't take me long to break off enough bars to create a hole in the kennel large enough for me to squeeze out. I was free! But I was also angry that they left me home alone. So, I went to the front door and attempted to open it. I chewed on the door frame and scratched the door with the toenails on my front paws. When the door didn't open—if it had, I had no idea where I would have gone—I found a large plastic storge container in the corner, and I began to chew on the edge of it. The lid popped off, and I gave it a good chewing and tearing before beginning on one corner of the container. Then, after getting tired of such play, I jumped on the bed. And even though Corbin and Dani let me sleep with them on the bed, I peed all over it in protest of being left alone. It reminded me of all the time I spent alone at Robert and Susan's house abandoned in the back yard, sometimes for several days at a time. When Corbin and Dani got home, they met them at the front door with my head leaning down. They knew what that meant. So, they asked, "What did you do?" And immediately, before I could answer, they saw the chewing on the door frame and spotted the pieces of plastic that had once been a storage container. As they began to clean up the mess I had made, one of them noticed the bed sheet and blanket all ruffled and wet, and they knew I had peed on them. They reprimanded me verbally, all the while I stood before them with my head slowly sinking onto the floor. When they stopped speaking to me, I went to the corner and lay down on the hardwood floor and watched as they tidied the apartment.

I figured that since the kennel had a hole in it, that my days in it were over. However, Corbin told Mark what I had done. He decided that he might be able to fix it. So, he came over to the apartment to get it and take it home with him. In the meantime, either Corbin or Dani took me for walks or to the dog park just a couple of blocks from the apartment. In the dog park, I could play with other dogs, unless I did something wrong and got put in detention until I was ready to behave again. The next time I saw my kennel, the hole I had created was patched with coat-hanger wire, and the whole kennel—top, bottom, and sides—was wrapped in small chicken wire fence, which was firmly attached to the kennel by picture-hanging wire. I listed as Mark explained to Corbin how he had spent all day fixing the kennel. "I repaired the hole with clothes-hanger wire by weaving it through the bars Shelby did not break," said Mark "Then, thinking that if she could not get her nose in between the bars, I put chicken wire all around it and anchored it to the kennel. If she cannot stick her nose through the bars because of the chicken wire, she cannot break out of the kennel." So, Corbin and Dani put the rug back in it, and told him, "We'll give it a try tomorrow, when both of us have to be gone."

The next day both of them left after putting me in the kennel. As soon as they were out the door, I began to study the chicken wire all around and on top and on the bottom. I figured out that chicken fence was made of a single, woven strand of wire. If I could find the right place and begin to tug and pull, I might undo some it. I found the place, and began to pull with my teeth. I got a section to unravel. Then, repeating the previous moves, I stuck my nose in, turned my head, and pushed the bars of the kennel apart. I worked a few cross bars until they broke off. Then more until I had a hole big enough for me to slide through. While I had the taste of galvanized chicken fence and black paint from the kennel bars in my mouth, I was free. I went to my bowl and got a drink of water. To sooth my anger, I chewed on the door again, found another plastic container to demolish, and jumped on the bed and peed! When Corbin and Dani opened the door, I greeted them with my head lowered. They looked around and saw what I had done and scolded me verbally. Corbin called Mark. I heard Corbin say: "She managed to get out again. The chicken wire didn't work. And she chewed on the door, destroyed another plastic container, and peed on the bed again. We don't know what to do."

A few days later, when both of them had to be gone again, I heard Corbin calling Mark and asking him, "Can you take Shelby for a while?" Then, Corbin took me to his car and drove me to Mark's house. He led me on the leash to the front porch, where Mark met us. Corbin handed the leash to Mark and, after telling him a few things about me, left me there. As soon as Mark left the room, I jumped into a big chair. He came back shortly and reprimanded me, making me get out of the chair. A while later, I went to his bedroom and jumped on the bed. It was soft and easy to lie on. He found me there and told me, "Get off. You will not lie on the furniture." His tone of voice told me that in his house my place was on the floor. Several times that first extended visit, he took me to the back yard to pee, even though I didn't need to pee that much. He came to find me several times in the house to be sure that I was not on the furniture. I went to his office a few times and put my paw on his knee to get petted. Then, I needed to poop. So, I went to his office and put both of my front paws on his knee, but he didn't know what that meant. He petted me and went back to what he was doing. I needed to poop really bad. So, I hopped down the steps to the basement and went as far back as I could, and I pooped on the floor. Then, I hopped up the steps and pretended like nothing had happened. I heard him tell Corbin a few days later that he had smelled poop in the basement but had not discovered it until two or three days later. For all practical purposes, that was my moving-in day to Mark's house.

Corbin was a musician, who played the guitar and several other instruments. He wrote songs. When he was working on music, I loved to lie at his feet and listen to him sing. It soothed me, and often I fell asleep. The studio apartment was not so bad as long as someone was there to be with me. However, after my previous behaviors, both Corbin and Dani knew that leaving me home alone would not work. Furthermore, the kennel was broken, so they could no longer put me in it. The only solution, was to find a place to take me, when both of them had to be away.

One day they took me with them to Corbin's parents' home. His parents had a dog with whom I played. As I have already mentioned, their dog had a green bone toy, which I liked. After playing with it one evening I took it to a tote bag belonging to Dani, and I dropped it into the bag. Corbin and Dani didn't find it until they got home. Of course, they wouldn't let me keep it! They brought it back to Corbin's parents' dog the next time they visited them. Mark bought me a green bone, but I wouldn't play with it; it just sat in my toy box in Mark's house. "You're a rascal," Mark said to me. 'It's the excitement of stealing the green bone that matters to you," he said to me.

5

MARK'S HOUSE

BECAUSE CORBIN AND DANI needed to be away from the studio apartment on the weekend, they began taking me to Mark's house on Saturday morning and gathering me on Sunday evening. Mark not only provided me with food, but he made a pallet on the floor near his bed upon which I could sleep. He had made it very clear that I was not to get on the furniture. He took me for a morning walk so I could pee and poop. In the afternoon, he took me for a two-mile walk, and I could explore and smell almost anything I could reach with my leash along our route. He reinforced the commands I already knew, and he added a few new ones which I learned quickly. "I knew you were a smart dog," he often said to me. As he treated me with more and more respect, in time, I returned the favor. What made him different is that he wanted to get to know me, and I decided I wanted to get to know him. So, we spent a lot of time with each other when I was at his house. He was always happy to see me, when Corbin and Dani brought me to his home. He even renamed me Shelbydog. It became his pet name for me. Because I got hot walking, he began to carry a bottle of water for me. We'd stop in the shade, and he would pour water into his left hand while holding the bottle in his right hand. I learned how to lap the water out of his hand. Often, I would spend two nights a week at his house.

During the summer of the year Corbin and Dani were living in the studio apartment and I spent most weekends at Mark's house, Corbin and Dani were gone for two weeks in June. Mark had volunteered to keep me, even though they wanted to put me in a boarding kennel. Because Mark had to be gone a part of the day, he put me in the backyard for the morning. He would come home for lunch and let me into the house, feed me, then put me back in the yard while he was gone for a few more hours in the afternoon. This was the first length of time that I spent every day at Mark's house. After what I had done in the studio apartment, he didn't trust me in the house alone. In order to be comfortable, I found a spot near the foundation of the house in the shade where the soil was soft. So, with all four paws I began excavation work. I worked on it for several days, unbeknown to Mark, enlarging it so my whole body would fit into the cool earth near the cool concrete. That's where I spent my time in the backyard sleeping and dreaming. However, as I was exploring the back yard one day, I noticed the back gate. After testing the soil under the back gate, I knew I was able to move enough of it out of the way to squeeze under it. The only problem were a few flat rocks which formed a walkway from one side of the gate to the other side. But with plenty of pull, I was able to move them enough over the excavated soil to create a tunnel deep enough for me to slither under the gate. And I was free. I didn't know what to do with my freedom, and I was tired from all the digging, so I went to the front steps of the house and lay down on the cool concrete. When Mark came home, he found me there. I greeted him with excitement. He said, "How did you get out?" He took the ring on my harness and led me through the garage to the backyard, which he inspected. He found the tunnel, and, while I watched, he filled it, replaced the flat walkway rocks, and piled pavers and bricks on them so that I would not be able to move them.

The next day, I was put into the backyard. I was so tired of digging from the previous day that I all I did was go to my hole and sleep most of the time I was there. Two days later, while exploring the backyard, I noticed there was a possible opening over the back gate. I knew I would not be able to move the heavy pavers, but I might be able to use them as leverage to get over the gate. After studying the chain-linked fence and chained-linked gate, I figured out where to put my paws and climb the gate to the open area, through which I squeezed and jumped down on the other side. I was free again, and I wanted in the house. So, I went to the sliding glass door that had a screen on it, and I jumped against it, getting my toenails caught in it and ripping it open. When that possibility for entry failed, I gave up and went back to the front steps, where Mark found me, when he got home. He repeated the process of a few days before; he led me by the ring on my harness through the garage and to the backyard. He walked the perimeter of the yard looking for tunnels, but he found none. He went to the back gate and saw what had been a small opening now larger and determined that was the way I got out. Getting pieces of siding and two-by-fours, he created a barrier along and over the gate that made it impossible for me to climb. Thus, I was back in the backyard in my hole for several more days.

Daydreaming, however, I got another idea. If I could climb the chain-linked gate, maybe I could climb the six-foot high, chain-linked fence. It took a lot of careful maneuvering, but I managed to get my feet in the right places and propel myself over the fence. The jump down caused me to crash and knock the wind out of me, but nothing was broken. So after a few moments, I got up and walked to the front porch steps. This time, the neighbor across the street saw me. She went to the next-door neighbor who had a key to the house. She opened the front porch door, and I walked in. Then, she locked the door. The door between the porch and the living room was shut and locked, so all I had was the front porch. But I was where I wanted to be, inside the house. When Mark came home and found me there, he called Corbin, asking, "When did you put Shelby on the front porch?" Corbin told him, "I didn't." Mark thought he had a magical dog until the neighbors came over and told him what had happened. This last escape made both Mark and Corbin aware that I would not destroy anything, as there were several shelves of books on the porch, and I didn't touch a single one.

After this, Corbin took me home with him for a few days. Mark was not home when he brought me back. He put me in the back yard in the hope that I would stay there long enough for Mark to return. However, when he went through the back door of the garage, he failed to close it tight enough for it to latch. After he left, I went and jumped against it, and it swung open. I went to the door connecting the garage to the house, but it was locked and would not open. I was furious at not being able to get into the house. I had already jumped on the screen of the garage window, ripping it open with my paws. Now, I took out my anger on the four gadgets that sent beams of light across the bottom of the two garage doors to keep them from coming down on something in the way. I bit into them, tearing off pieces of them and ripping wires and putting out their red lights. Then, I began to bite the hard plastic handle on the chest freezer, until I got pieces of it to break lose. When Mark got home, he was very upset at the damage I did, and he called Corbin, saying, "Come over and see what damage your dog did because you didn't close the door until it latched."

Meanwhile, Corbin went out and bought a woven wire leash that one end could be attached to a tree in Mark's backyard and the other attached to my collar. Because of my ability to climb the fence, Corbin thought that I would have to be tied, and Mark agreed. So, before he left, Mark took me outside and hooked me to the end of the wire leash. I absolutely hated being tied. I went into a fit. Before Mark could get back into the house, I had backed up and let the collar slip off my head. I didn't know that he was watching me from the window. He came back outside, took the collar and put it around my neck and tightened it a notch or two. He left, and I tried to get it off, but it was too tight. I began to chew on a small holly tree, tearing off branches. I bit the side of a storage shed, ripping off small pieces of wood. Mark, who was watching me through the window, came outside and took me off the wire leash. He said to me, "I can't do this to you." And he let me come into the house and onto the front porch. That is where I was left with a bowl of water. The door into the living room was closed, but I had gotten to where I wanted to be. Both Mark and Corbin now knew I was trustworthy.

The front porch became my room. Mark and Corbin would leave me there all the time. Of course the door into the living room and the rest of the house was closed. Nevertheless, I had a room, and the full glass door let in stream after stream of sunshine in which I bathed on a daily basis. Because Mark was a walker, on most afternoons we hiked for two miles. I got to know the neighborhood, especially where all the cats lived! During the seventh year of my life, Mark bought me a bed to replace the pallet upon which I had been sleeping. He placed the bed on the floor next to his bed.

That way I knew he was near, even at night. Sometimes, when I was having a bad dream, he would place his hand on me and gently awaken me. If I got up during the night to stretch or get a drink of water, when I came back, I'd put my paw on his bed to awaken him. He would lean over and pet me and talk to me before I lay down, curled up, and went back to sleep. He bought me a couple bandanas to wear. I had one or two that I had received when getting a bath and nail trim at the pet store, but I liked the ones he gave me. In a few months, some of his friends brought me six more bandanas I began to wear a bandana every day. People in the neighborhood got to know me that way, and I got to know them.

After Corbin and Dani left the studio apartment, they moved to a one-room house fifty miles away. They knew they could not leave me there all day long. So, except for a few times a month, when they took me home with them for a day or two before bringing me back to Mark, I was becoming Mark's dog. Besides walking me and feeding me, he began to undo some of my response to various things. For example, because I had been beaten with sticks and wooden handles by Robert and Susan, anytime Mark went by me with a broom or mop or shovel or hoe, I would dunk as if I were going to get hit. Mark would see this take place, and say, "I'm not going to hurt you, Shelbydog." This scenario repeated itself over and over again until I trusted and learned that, indeed, he was not going to hit me. When walking and seeing men working, I would look at their shoes and back away if they resembled Robert's shoes. Again, I learned that they were not going to kick me and began to approach them and let them pet me. Because I had been sprayed with a hose, I stayed away when Mark had a garden hose in the backyard. He had bought me a small pool to get into and cool off. I loved lying in the water on a warm day. If the hose was still in the pool, I would not get in. After Mark figured out what was going on, he began to take the hose away from the pool so I could get in the water and enjoy it. He kept telling me, "Nothing is going to hurt you, Shelbydog."

Because I had been left out in the thunder, lightning, and rain, I was so scared when it thundered that I would leave the front porch and go to my bed and hide. Sometimes I would find Mark and lie at his feet. He began to call me to go with him to the front porch. I would sit in front of the full glass door and he would kneel behind me and put his arm around me, saying, "It's not going to hurt you, sweetie." A thunder clap would be heard and I would tremble while he held me and repeated, "It's not going to hurt you. I won't let anything hurt Shelbydog." While three years later I continue to enter the house most of the time when I hear thunder or see lightning, many times I stay on the porch because I know that it is not going to hurt me.

Mark has worked with me for a long time. He had gotten to know me and the sign language I speak. He could read the expressions on my face and tell by my posture what I needed. He called it dog psychology. I call it love and respect. He loves me, kissing me on the head several times a day, but especially in the morning and in the evening when he prays with and for me. He respects me enough to help me grow out of the bad experiences I had for the first five years of my life. He welcomes me to a new day, saying to me when I get up, "Good morning, Madam Shelbydog!" He puts me to bed at night, praying with and for me and kissing me good night, saying, "Know how much I love you," before pulling a blanket over me. As soon as I am covered, I begin to drift off into peaceful, restful, and secure sleep. Several times an evening, he will lean over from his bed and pull my blanket over me after I have twisted and turned during the night.

Since I came to Mark's house, I've experienced two incidents that prompted me to nip two people. On one occasion Mark had a friend of his named Art visiting for a few days. One morning in semi-darkness he entered quietly the kitchen where my food and water bowls were located and caught me off guard. I protected my place by nipping him on the thigh. He said I bit him, because I did draw a tiny bit of blood. On another occasion, Corbin took me to a family gathering. I was sitting beside him. His cousin came over, and I perceived that he was coming to hit me. So, I grabbed his arm. Corbin slapped me to make me turn loose of him. I had no intention of really biting him; I wanted only to stop what I perceived to be an attack. I used to follow and nip a lot of people in order to get their attention. But as I began to understand that they thought I was attempting to bite them, I stopped. Now I just stand in front of people and wag my tail in the hope that they will pet me and give me attention.

While living with Mark during the seventh year of my life, I got to know the mail carrier named Jared. When Jared first introduced himself to me, I was not interested in getting to know him. Usually, he was delivering mail in the neighborhood when Mark took me for a walk after lunch. He would come to me, sometimes having to cross the street to do so, and talk to me and pet me. Then, he would go on delivering mail. He continued this behavior for about three months. He won me over. I began to look for his mail truck when Mark and I were out walking; I could tell it was his by smelling the door. His scent was inside. I began to lie on my side or roll over for him to give me belly rubs. If I were on the front porch when he arrived with mail, I would pick up my cloth duckie toy, while Mark opened the glass door, and bring it out to him. He would take it from my mouth and tease me with it. Sometimes he would throw up in the air and I would catch it. Other times, he would just stand in the driveway and play with me. For two years, when on walks with Mark, I would look for Jared and/or his truck, and I would look forward to his visit to see me and play with me. I was sad for a few days after he accepted a transfer in the post office department, but he has stopped by to see me several times. His replacements have become my friends. Mark has trained them, saying, "She won't hurt you. Just take her duckie from her and give it back." A few of them will even pet me. Nevertheless, I still miss Jared, because he truly got to know me and to understand me.

6

NEW PERMANENT HOME

HERE IS A SUMMARY: I am Shelbydog, a sixty-pound, brindle Labrador-Boxer mix. I am ten years old, born April 7, 2012. I am living in my third home. My first home was with Robert and Susan, and they were abusive. They took me away from the kennel where I was born when I was eight weeks old to their house, where I experienced beatings, kickings, hose-sprayings, and I was left outside in the rain, thunder, and lightning. After four years of abuse and having bitten Susan, Robert and Susan moved to a new city and they took me to the local dog shelter and left me there. I was in that shelter for six months, but, because no one would adopt me, I was transported to another shelter, where I lived for six more months. All of my fifth year of life was spent in a shelter. My second home was with Corbin and Dani, although it was very fluid. During my sixth and seventh years of life, I lived in an apartment with four other men, then in a studio apartment, then in a one-room house, but most of the time with Mark. Mark's home became at first another fluid place for me to live, but then it became my third permanent home, where I have lived during my eighth through tenth years of life. Now, I return to my story.

During the summer of my seventh year of life, Corbin and Dani moved to a single-room home about fifty miles away from Mark's house. That meant that most of the time I lived with Mark. Now and then Corbin and Dani would take me home with them for a Friday night and bring me back to Mark's house on Saturday afternoon. While I liked spending time with Corbin, listening to him play guitar music and sing the songs upon which he was working, and spending time with Dani, as she brushed me and talked to me, my real home now was with Mark. In late August as the days were getting shorter, I would often leave my post on the front porch and go to bed, sometimes as early at 7 p.m. or 7:30 p.m. I remember one evening when that occurred. Later, when Mark came into the bedroom, I got out of my bed and lay spread eagle on the floor, because I was hot. Mark, who had just gotten ready to get into his bed, saw me and understood what I was saying. So, he went over to the window air conditioner, turned it on, shut the bedroom door, and climbed into his bed. I got up off the floor and went back to my bed. The message was delivered and received! Both of us slept well that night.

It wasn't long after that when Mark understood something else I had to say. He had come into the living room to watch the local evening news. I left the front porch, where I was lying on a rug in front of the all-glass door, and went to his chair, putting my paw on his knee. He petted my head and scratched my belly—thinking that was what I wanted—and I got up and went back to the porch. A few minutes later, I went back to him. He sat on the floor by me, and I began to paw him with my left foot, then the right foot, then the left foot again. He understood then that I wanted to go outside for a walk. I went and sat on the rug by the door facing outside and waiting for him to get my leash and take me. A couple of minutes later, he was ready to go.

Some days when it is hot, I don't want to go for a walk after lunch. I like to lie on the tile floor on the front porch where it is cool. "Do you want to go for a walk?" Mark will ask me. I reply by raising my head just a little and looking at him over the back of my head and then quickly putting it down again, basically saying, "No!" He usually comes back later asking me the same thing. If I've changed my mind, I get up and look like I am ready to go.

In August of my seventh year of life, a very loud thunderstorm came through after 11 p.m. I was sleeping deeply when the thunder awakened me and I could see the lightning flashes behind the window blinds. I pawed Mark's bed, and that awakened him. He petted me and told me, "Nothing is going to hurt you." I lay on my bed for about a minute. However, the thunder was loud and the lightning continued to flash. So, Mark got up and we went to the front door of the porch, and I sat down while he knelt down behind me. We could see the rain and the lightning flashes and hear the thunder. He kept repeating, "Nothing is going to hurt you." Finally, I stopped shaking and calmed down. We continued that posture for a long time in the silent darkness of the night, except for the noisy rain and thunder. Then, we went back to bed and back to sleep.

At this point in time, I was eating a lot of food from the table. My favorite food was cheese, especially cheddar. I had a variety of kibble, chicken with vegetables and lamb with rice. Mark also bought me a variety of soft, canned food. Add in the trachea pieces and at least three kinds of Milk Bones, and I had an ever-changing diet. I remember one night when Mark was scrambling eggs with cheese and mushrooms. After he finished cooking it, he put a few spoons of it in my food bowl. It smelled good. So I stuck out my tongue and tasted the eggs only to discover that they were good but too hot. So, I moved away from the bowl and walked around the kitchen. I returned and tasted the food again, but it was still too hot. So, I walked around the kitchen again. Mark watched me do this dance around my food bowl and laughed. Finally, the eggs had cooled enough for me to eat them, and I wasted no time in eating all of them and licking my bowl to be sure I left nothing in it.

Mark and I used to walk two miles in the afternoon. In those days of the seventh year, the heat and humidity didn't both me as much as they do today. Mark would carry a bottle of water for me, and after walking about half a mile, we would stop under a shade tree along the sidewalk. I would lie on the cool grass, and he would pour water into his left hand while holding the bottle in his right. I would lap it out of his hand. After a few minutes, we would walk some more. In the park we walked around, there was a stone bench, where we took another break. I'd lay spread eagle on the bench with my front paws hanging over the end, while Mark gave me water to drink from his hand. Because we stopped on the bench on a regular basis, I expected the water bottle to appear, while I stretched on the cool stone of the bench. Mark would often say, "I can hear the water gurgling in your tummy." The stone bench felt really cool on my belly! On our way home from the bench in the park we often passed a wood fence. I always headed toward it because I liked to rub my back along it from one end to the other and back again. Then, I would fall to the ground and roll and wiggle and role and wiggle my way down the hill. I would get up, rub myself against the fence, and roll and wiggle again. Finally, I would get up and shake off all the debris that had clung to me, and we would continue on the way home. Mark understood how important it was for me to rub my back on that fence and let me play roll-and-wiggle down the hill.

Once I discovered how much Mark cared for me, I lost my fear of getting beaten with a stick or handle of a broom, mop, or hoe. I stopped dunking when he went by with any such item in his hand. He could step over me with such items, and I wouldn't move. I trusted him. So, I tried very hard to communicate with him. I would go to the kitchen and sit on the rug in front of the sink. He began to understand that there was some food item that I wanted. His job was to figure out which item it was! If he gave me the wrong item, I would just drop it on the floor. He'd pick it up and put it away, and then he would get something else. Once I kept it in my mouth and went to my favorite rug to eat it, he knew he figured out what I wanted. Sometimes, if it wasn't the correct item, I would turn up my nose or not take it at all. When I wanted him to give me a belly rub, I would bring him a piece of my rawhide bone and lead him to the rug in the living room. I'd lie down and roll over with all four feet up in the air. He'd scratch my belly until I got up and left. At other times I'd lead him to the glass door on the front porch and sit. He knew to kneel behind me and pet me while I watched cars and he talked to me. "You are so pretty," he'd say. Or he would point out cars to me: "There goes a red car. Look! There is a blue car. Look over there at the white car!" I loved our time together.

In my sixth year of life, when Mark was taking me for a walk one morning, we got about two blocks from home and my right, back leg locked up. I couldn't move. He took a few steps forward, but I couldn't follow him. After thinking for a few minutes, he said, "I don't know what to do." But then he put his arms under my belly and lifted me up from the earth, holding me close to himself. He walked by two houses and had to sit me down. He rested for a few minutes and then picked me up again and walked past two or three more houses. I was in pain; Mark knew because I didn't even wiggle when he picked me up. We repeated this process until we got home, and he carried me up the steps and put me on the front porch. Since in those days I was still Corbin's dog, he called Corbin and explained what had happened to me. Corbin called my veterinarian, who told him to go to a pet store and by Cosequin, a joint health supplement for dogs, for me. He was instructed to give me two tablets a day for thirty days and after that one a day. Mark made me a soft pallet to lie upon on the front porch. After Corbin arrived, he gave me two Cosequin tablets. And I could feel the difference within the hour. I began to walk into the house and was able to go outside that evening to pee. The next day, there was little to no pain. And the day after that, I wanted to play again. The pain in my joints was and is caused by the spaying that was done to me.

In my seventh year, I had been taking Cosequin, wrapped in soft dog food, for about a year. I decided that I didn't need it anymore, since I could walk two miles easily except for the need to take a break or two due to the heat and humidity. Mark would place the tablet concealed by soft dog food on the top of the food in my bowl, and I would take it. Once I decided differently, I refused to take it by eating around it or I just didn't eat the food in my bowl. Some days I wouldn't eat until the evening, when I would take my medicine and eat my food. I was going through some strange process! I know I made Mark very upset and afraid when I wouldn't take my medicine or eat. I remember one day after our morning walk when he prepared the medicine for me. He presented it to me, and I turned my head and walked away. Using a very stern voice, he said, "Shelby, come back and take this medicine NOW." I had come to understand that the use of the word NOW meant immediate action required. That day, I came back and took the Cosequin.

The next day, I repeated the scenario of not taking my medicine. Mark said, "I'm very disappointed in you, Shelby. I can't tell you how sad I am." I hung my head and walked to my bed and lay down with my head as low as possible. I know Mark felt bad about this kind of conflict between us, and I felt bad for being so stubborn. He came into the bedroom and apologized to me, giving me a belly rub, hugging me, and telling me, "I love you." A little later, I went into the kitchen and found my bowl with food and medicine and ate all of it. The rest of the day I was on good behavior and very cooperative. The last Sunday of August in 2019, I watched Mark prepare my food with the medicine on top. He didn't say anything to me about it, because he didn't like handling the stress of us being at odds with each other. I took my medicine and ate my food. Then, he took me to a trail, where we walked for two and half miles. I was able to get into a small stream that ran along the trail; I loved getting into the water to cool. I was as cooperative as I could be that day and for the rest of the week. And I'm glad I did because that night a loud thunderstorm with rain and lightning came through. I awakened Mark with my paw on the bed, and he reassured me that nothing was going to hurt me. He patted my head for a while. Then, he got up and led me to the front door, where I sat and he knelt behind me watching the rain and lightning and listening to the thunder. He kept saying, "Nothing is going to hurt you."

He used the same words—"Nothing is going to hurt you"—when my allergies were bad and before my vet put me on Claritin. In the morning when I got up, a lot of crusty eye discharge was in the corner of my eyes during spring and fall. Mark would take a tissue and gently clean away the discharge. While doing so, he would keep repeating, "I'm not going to hurt you." After he did this a few times, I trusted him not to poke me in the eye. My instinct was to turn my head away from him and close my eyes, but after hearing "I'm not going to hurt you," I would merely close my eyes and let him clean them.

Mark bought me small inflatable pool. He inflated it, put it in the back yard, and filled it with water. One day after our afternoon walk, he took me to the filled pool, and I got in it immediately and loved it. I was able to lie down in it with the water covering my back, but not my head. The cool water felt so good on my skin. Mark said to me, "This is better than the creek along the trail that has all the chemical runoff from people's yards in it." After I would get out, on my way into the house I'd stop in the garage and hop onto a bench, and Mark would take a towel and dry me from nose to tail. He would pick up each of my feet and dry between my toes so that I wouldn't slide so much on the tile floors in the house. After drying me off, he would hug me and kiss me on the head. Then, I would jump down and head into the house for a nap. Because the pool was easily punctured with my toenails, he had to repair it several times. I remember him taking me to it a couple of times, only to discover that all the water had drained out. I was disappointed, and he would say, "I'm so sorry, sweetie." Ultimately, he bought me a small pool made out of hard plastic, and my toenails could not puncture it. I used it often until Mark discovered that the water was drying my sensitive skin.

One day while he was toweling me, Mark said, "I've gotten to know you, Shelbydog. You are unique, and I love you. Your brindle color with red highlights makes you like a burning bush of divine presence for me. You are my special friend." His love for me was attested by the good-night prayer, hug, and kiss I always got. My owner, Corbin, shared me with Mark, and I'm so happy he did. My relationship with Mark had grown, just like his relationship with Corbin. Having my two favorite people present with me made me be evermore present to them and gave me twice the opportunity to get belly rubs!

When the day was hot and humid, Mark took me for a mile walk early in the morning. If he worked outside after lunch, I would stay inside where the air conditioning was. The humidity really affected my physical ability. I remember waiting for him in the kitchen. When I saw him coming in, I would lead him to the front porch and lie on my side for a belly rub. Because he needed a shower after working outside, he would make the belly rub short. After his shower he would go to the living room, and there I'd be waiting for him on the large rug. Often, he would lie by me on the rug and scratch my belly, while I rolled from side to side or arched my back and stopped with all my feet in the air to feel the scratching better. Outside, I was well known for what Mark called my drop-and-roll routine. When I was hot and wanted to stop and rest, I'd throw myself onto the ground and roll and wiggle, feeling the cool grass and earth against my fur. After a minute or two of this, I'd stand up, shake myself, and continue the walk.

I also had an uncanny ability to find interesting things along the sidewalk, especially cats! I couldn't keep my nose away from smells on the ground or in the air. The smells I wanted to investigate were always as far away as possible from the sidewalk. I would pull and pull the leash to get to a tree trunk or bush, and I'd often get lost in whatever I was investigating until Mark would tug the leash calling me to resume our walk. I remember Mark saying one morning, "I don't think the world is big enough for you, Shelby" One morning he told me: "You are a mystical dog. You lose your sense of place, just following your nose. You'd walk right out into the traffic if I didn't have you on a leash. When I give you a belly rub, you arch your back and stick all your feet into air, while your eyes roll back, and you enter into ecstasy." On another occasion, he told me: "You watch the cars pass on the busy street; you growl at walkers and joggers as they pass by; you bark at cats; you stretch out and sleep. You are mesmerized by car lights. What a special dog you are."

In September of my seventh year, Corbin married Dani. While they were living about fifty miles away from Mark, I stayed most of the time with Mark. However, on their wedding day I lost a dog friend named Hank Williams. Dani had gotten him as a puppy from her father; he was the last of the litter to go. He was only about six months old, but he had grown up some under my watchful eyes. In fact, he was the same size as I. As I heard Corbin tell Mark what had happened—he had jumped to his death out of the bed of a moving pick-up truck—I was sad. My sadness didn't last too long, however. Mark was responsible for bringing me to the wedding. When I got there, I knew a lot of the people who were present. I got overly excited, and Mark took me to a quite spot in the kitchen until the ceremony was ready to begin. Once he took me into the church, he gave me a rawhide bone to chew on to keep me still. After the ceremony, I mingled with other people I knew at the reception. On the way back to Mark's house, I slept all the way home in the back seat.

Living with Mark in the quiet of his home and going to that noisy wedding has made me aware that I am an introvert. I like being alone on the front porch. I like being alone in my bed in the bedroom. I like being alone outside when lying in the sun; and, when I get too hot, lying in the shade. While it is nice to walk and meet people on the sidewalks, it is also nice to be alone. I think Mark and I understand this truth deeply. That is why one of us finds the other a couple of times a day, spends a few minutes with each other, and then goes back to whatever we were doing.

Something I appreciate that Mark does for me is cover me at night. I love to sleep with a blanket totally covering me from nose to tail. I curl up when Mark puts me to bed, and he spreads the blanket over me. Within seconds I am in deep sleep. When he awakens during the night, he always leans over and pulls my blanket over me. I move a lot during the night. It is not uncommon for me to fall asleep in one direction and awaken in another direction. So, when Mark rolls over, he grabs my blanket—sometimes having to pull it out from under me—and covers me. I've discovered that when it is hot outside, both of us like to sleep in the cool the air conditioner provides.

In the morning and the evening I like to look for rabbits when we walk. I smell where they have been and explore the area. Over the years, I have found a few. I remember smelling one near a bush. When I stuck my nose into the bush, the rabbit jumped out and ran away. He so startled me that I jumped back. I also remember finding a rabbit in his den under a big rock near a sidewalk. Every morning I would step toward the rock and smell the rabbit, who would quickly jump out and run away. Because I was on a leash, I was not able to pursue him, but I liked finding rabbits.

The trust I had for Mark continued to grow. I trusted him to clean my eyes, to dry me with a towel after being in my pool, to feed me, to water me, to play with me. I know it humbled him for me to be so trustworthy. We extended respect to each other. He was concerned that Corbin was losing his connection to me because of all the time I spent at Mark's house. I remember him telling Corbin, "She is your dog, but she and I are bonding." And that was very true. Over the course of two years, we had grown in mutual respect for each other. He had taught me many things I didn't know, and I had returned the favor. He didn't know that he could love a dog, but I believed he could. He did not disappoint me. When I went with Corbin and Dani to their studio apartment or their one-room house for a day or two, I always looked forward to being brought back to Mark's house, where I had a bed that was mine and a room, the front porch, that was mine to watch cars and people pass by.

The death of Hank Williams at so young an age really affected me, and I know it affected Mark, too. I thought about how short a dog's life is in human years. Mark considered how he would feel and respond if something happened to me. I'm not sure, but I think the death made Mark love me more. He spent more time with me. Even when workers were installing a new furnace in his house and I wanted to be there to watch what they were doing, he put on my leash and took me to a place out of the way but where I could see them. We sat together and watched everything unfold before us. I couldn't help myself; ever so often I just had to get up, go over to where they were, and smell the guys and the stuff they were using. I got a lot of petting as I brought them my rawhide bone. Mark had to explain, "Take the bone from her and then give it back. It is her gift to you."

By the middle of September I was at home in Mark's house. He had tried to play with me, but I wasn't yet in the mood. Finally, one day he picked up my rawhide bone. I saw him and tried to take it away from him. When he got back from grocery shopping, I ran to greet him at the back door with the bone. I was so excited that he was home and not abandoning me that I could barely contain myself, as I ran up the steps and through the house and back to him. I wanted to welcome him home, to the home he shared with me. I dared to hope that this would be my permanent home for the rest of my life.

"Shelby is a very messy drinker and eater," Mark told his friend Dan, as they were setting up the garage for a yard sale. "I have to keep a rug under her bowls. And even then, she manages to splash water on the floor and leave small pieces of her food on the rug and on the floor." The first time Dan saw me, he liked me, and I liked him. I watched him and Mark prepare the tables in the garage with all kinds of things that I went and smelled. Then, for two days after that I spent my time in the garage with them as they conducted their annual garage sale. I lay between their chairs where I could see the driveway. As customers began to arrive, I began to growl at them. Mark kept telling, "Shelby, stop growling at the customers." A few times all he said when I growled was "Shelby! Shelby!" I got it: I stopped growling, and I discovered that many of the customers would come to me and pat me on the head or rub my ears or scratch my belly. I enjoyed all that attention. Dan enjoyed me, too, and petted me often. He also spoke to me a lot. Because I learned so quickly to stop growling, after supper Mark came to kneel behind me, while I sat, on the front porch. We did that for a long time. He would talk to me, saying, "What a good girl you are. I love you, Shelby. Thank You for behaving today." I would relax and lean against him while he rubbed by head, ears, and front leg joints and we watched cars and people go by.

When I was at his house, I didn't have to get up when he did. He often awakened around 5 to 5:30 in the morning. I would continue to sleep until 8 or 9 a.m. He had often finished his morning routine by the time I got up, stretched several times, and went to the front porch to see what was happening in my world. When he had errands to run, he would usually take me with him. All he had to say was, "Shelby, do you want to go for a ride?" I would become so excited that I couldn't be still until he opened the car door and I jumped into the back seat. Some places we went I was able to go in as long as I was on my leash. Other places I had to wait in the car. While I liked going into stores and experiencing all the smells in every aisle and on every shelf, I knew I was not permitted in some stores. One of my favorite stores was the hardware one, where the cashier always gave me a handful of treats. In the car, sometimes I would sit in the back seat and watch the world go by; other times I would stretch out and lie on the seat and enjoy the rocking motion of the car as it slowed and stopped at red lights and then rolled again when the lights turned green.

I became very happy living with Mark. I liked getting into the water in my pool in the backyard. I liked dropping and rolling in the grass on walks. I remember Mark saying, "It is your expression of pure joy! I watch in wonder and share your joy!" I demonstrated joy to an old man at the end of the street; one of his dogs died. One day when Mark and I were walking, he was walking his other dog. I went to her and rubbed noses with her, saying, "I am sorry that your friend passed away." I was very happy when Corbin came to see me. He would play with me for a long time and lie on the floor and talk to me. I remember one time when Mark was concerned about me not eating all my food or only eating dinner. Corbin showed him some pictures of me after he had rescued me from the shelter. I was very skinny; you could see my ribs. Since then I had put on some weight. Corbin said, "I think she is not eating all her food because she is at the weight she needs to be." While that was not accurate, as will be explained below, it satisfied Mark for a while.

During that visit by Corbin, Mark also asked him about the shaking or shivering he had observed in me, when I was lying on the floor near him. Corbin thought it was due to me not eating and getting cold. Again, that was not totally accurate. Some of the shaking or shivering was the result of the abuse I had experienced the first four years of my life. In time, with love and care, it would disappear. I demonstrated to Mark how much I appreciated all the love and care he was giving me one day when Corbin came to get me and take me to the studio apartment. I was excited to see him, and I played with him and Mark in the living room. At one point, I went to Mark and placed my head on his knee and looked at him. I was saying, "I love you." He was very touched by my behavior. Corbin said, "Awe, how sweet," as he saw what I was doing. I know Mark misses me when I go spend a day or two with Corbin and Dani. One day when I was being picked up later in the day, he said, "Tonight I will be Shelbydogless!" I will never forget those words.

Another cute thing I did one day was get up and wander around the house until I was ready to go for my morning walk. Finally, I went to Mark in his office and put my paw on his knee; that was the way I told him, "I'm ready for my walk." He said, "Go sit on your rug, and I'll be right there." So, I went to my rug and sat in the opposite direction; my tail was toward Mark and my head was pointed to the way out of the house. He tried to get me to turn around, but I wouldn't budge. So, he got up and moved in front of me so he could put on my harness. After putting the collar part of the harness over my head, he said, "I need a foot," while touching my left foot and lifting it into the strip on the harness. Then, he said, "I need another foot," while touching my right foot and lifting it into the strip on the harness. Once he tightened the harness behind my head, he reached for a bandana and said, "Let's put on your pretty." I lower my head and let him slip on. Then, we are ready to walk. "You're ready," he says, and I go to the front door. I knew he was growing deeper and deeper in love with me. However, I was growing deeper and deeper in love with him. "You are my burning bush," he would say. "You are the divine presence to me."

7

ADVENTURES WITH MARK

By the end of September of my seventh year of life, I was happily living with Mark and visiting Corbin and Dani occasionally. Also, I was beginning to have some stomach issues. I didn't know it then, but eating all the different things that Corbin and Dani and Mark gave me were not good for me. Some of it gave me diarrhea. I remember one night on the last day of September 2019, awakening Mark at 11 p.m. to take me outside to the backyard, where I pooped and peed. I awakened him again at 2 a.m. to do the same things. And again at 6 a.m. While in the backyard at 2 a.m., I found some feces—cat or squirrel or something else—that really smelled good, and I rolled around in it. Mark didn't notice when I came in. However, when it went to put on my harness at 7:30 a.m., he smelled it and felt it dried on my fur. He decided that I needed a bath; this is the first bath that Mark gave me. Corbin had told him how much I hated baths, and I did not fail to live up to my reputation!

Before our morning walk, Mark called me into the kitchen, and I came. Then, he tried to get me into the bathroom, but I would not go. So, he rolled me over and picked me up by putting my front feet in one of his hands and my back feet in his other hand. I was upside down while he carried me the short distance to the bathroom and lay me down in the shower. He kept talking to me, telling me, "Stay!" and "Stop wiggling!" and "I'm not going to hurt you." All the while he kept a hand on me to keep me still while he took the shower head and wetted me. Then, he took his strawberry shampoo and squeezed it onto me all along my head and back to my tail. Taking some in his hands he put it on my legs. Repeatedly, he massaged me with the shampoo all over until I was just a pile of suds with four legs sticking out. Then, he rinsed me off and dried me with a towel. Then, we went for a walk, and my poop was soft. When we got back, I protested the bath by not taking my medicine at first. But because I was hungry, I took it and ate some of my food. Our post-lunch walk that day was only two blocks long because of the humidity and heat.

Every day Mark would take me for a two-mile walk. We would stop in the grass under a tree, and he would give me a drink of water from the bottle he carried for me. I would lap it out of his hand and then roll over and over in the grass in joy and abandon. On the way home, I looked forward to rubbing my back on a wood fence, then rolling down the hill in happiness. One evening when telling Corbin about this, Mark shared with him an insight. Corbin had said that I had become Mark's companion. Mark said: "The word *companion* means to share bread with another. And that is what I do. I give Shelbydog a few bites of whatever I'm eating on the top of her food. She often sits on the kitchen rug and waits for me to share some of my food with her. The way we share our lives is mirrored in the way we share our food!"

In mid-October it was still very hot at Mark's house. One evening after a walk I went to my pool and sat in it for a while. Then, I came into the garage and jumped on the bench. Mark dried me off and opened the door from the garage to the house. My feet were still damp when I jumped off the bench and headed up the steps into the house. I slipped and hit my head on the post supporting the steps and knocked myself unconscious for a few seconds. Mark heard the bang and came instantly to see what was happening. When he got to me, I was coming back to consciousness but really stunned, slipping off the steps and unable to move. He didn't know if I had hurt myself or not. He picked me up and took me to the top of the steps in the kitchen. Then, he put me down gently on the floor and I was able to take a few steps. "I think you are OK," he said to me. I walked to the front porch and lay down. He checked on me a couple times during the evening, but I was fine.

At this time in my life, I went on three walks a day. I had a short one in the morning and evening to pee and poop. I had a long one after lunch. While walking, Mark often said, "There is never enough leash for Shelbydog." What he meant was that I always wanted to explore a bush, a tree, a leaf, anything away from the sidewalk. This was also the time in my life when I was getting more and more unable to deal with the afternoon humidity and heat. One day in late October I had stopped abruptly on the way home because I was hot; my tongue was hanging out of my mouth! I planted all four of my feet even though Mark kept saying, "Shelby, let's go." I stayed, but he moved on with his back to me. I turned toward him and let the harness slip off my head; then, I stepped out of the straps around by front legs. When he turned to see why the leash was no longer taut, I ran across the street and headed home; we were about two blocks from home. I would run a little ahead and turn around and look at him, and run farther. A few times I even came back toward him and ran around him and then back toward home. After doing this several times and having so much fun, I got tired and hot and stopped and waited for him to come and put the harness back on me. I knew he was scared that I would run into the street and get hit by a passing car, but I knew better. So, I stayed on lawns or on the islands in front of them. When Mark caught up to me, he was laughing. He said to me, "You are so funny, but we need to put on your harness." I cooperated.

One day while Mark was lying on the rug by me and scratching my back and belly, he asked me: "If you could talk, what you say? What would you say about the first four years of your life? about your owners for those four years? about your year in shelters? about your life with Corbin and

Dani in two different apartments and a one-room house? about your life with me? about your favorite food? about the high points of your life? about the low points of your life? about why you solicit belly rubs so often? about how you feel on given days? about where are your favorite places to walk?" As I listened to him repeat question after question, I began to think about writing this book. He had just outlined it for me!

Finally, the October summer turned to October fall of 2019. The forty-degree day restored my energy. On our after-lunch walk, I wanted to run and play. I walked the two-miles fast, and only stopped long enough on the stone bench in the park to get a drink. When I wanted to play, I'd bring Mark a rawhide bone or a piece of one. I'd drop it on the floor and hunker down with my head and front legs on the floor, like I was ready to spring into action. All he had to do was make a move, and I'd grab the bone and run to the front porch or the large rug in the living room. Once he caught up with me, he would pet me and scratch my belly. I would kiss (lick) his hand. If he stopped, I'd stick my nose under his hand and lift it up; he knew that meant I wanted more petting and scratching to take place. When there is no sun shining, I do this several times a day!

By the end of October, Mark said, "Shelbydog is just being silly." I would find him, usually at his desk, and put my front paw on his knee after sitting up straight beside him. I was very good on both long and short walks. I was getting along with other dogs; however, I don't like small barking dogs. I turn around and walk away without a single bark. I had a new friend, named Barbara, whom I liked to visit. When walking in the area, I would pull Mark toward Barbara's house and trot up the back steps. Mark would ring the doorbell, and I would place my head close to the door to hear if Barbara was approaching to open the door. If she were home, she would open the door and invite us in, and I would begin to explore the den and kitchen of her home. Then, Barbara would give me three crackers and a glass bowl of water. I would lay on her slate kitchen floor and lap water. If Barbara didn't come to the back door, I'd pull Mark to the front door, where he would ring the bell, and I would stand with my ear to the door to listen for her footsteps within. Of course, at that time I did not understand that if she were not at one door, she would not be at the other one!

That fall, I spent a lot of time outside with Mark. I was free of a leash. He taught me that I was not permitted to cross the sidewalk in front of his house, but all the driveway and front yard were mine. So, while he was doing fall yard work—raking leaves, cleaning flower beds, etc.—I found places where the sun was shining and lay down there until I got hot. Then, I would move to a cooler place, then back to the sunshine. I loved being outside and free in the cool fall air. Mark told me, "You have been very cooperative and good." I would look at him and smile.

Inside, I went to bed every night between 5 and 6 p.m. Once darkness descended, I was ready for bed. Now and then I would lie on the rug in the living room at Mark's feet, while he sat in a chair watching TV. He would get out of his chair and sit on the rug near me. It thrilled me when he did that. I had a blanket and pillow on the rug, and he would raise my head and put my pillow under my head and cover me with the blanket. Then, he would pet me gently, scratch my belly, and leave his hand on my side, while I fell asleep and snored. Mark told me, "You snore very loud!" Both he and I loved to share those special moments. Later in the evening, he would awaken me, saying, "Shelby, it's time to go to bed." He'd have to say it several times because it takes me a while to gather enough energy to get up from sleep. I heard Mark tell Corbin one time, "I love to hear Shelbydog snoring near me."

On Christmas Eve, after we had gone to bed, Mark had a head cold and his sinuses were clogged and he couldn't breathe. He got up around 2 a.m. Christmas morning and went to sleep in a chair in the living room, as he had done the night before. Around thirty minutes after he settled into the chair, I got up to go see about him. In the dark and quiet of the night, the click, click, click of my toenails on the tile floor echoed through the house. When I got to the living room, I went to his chair and put my paw on his leg. He turned on the lamp and petted me. "Go back to bed," he said. Being obedient, I clicked, clicked, clicked my way back to the bedroom and lay on my bed for ten minutes before getting up and going back to Mark. With my paw on his knee again I told him to come back to bed. He followed me to the bedroom, where I got back into my bed and he got back into his. He leaned over and pulled the blanket over me, and both of us went back to sleep next to each other.

Another thing I like to do after Mark puts on my harness and bandana is sit on the rug in the middle of the front porch. There I can look outside through the glass door while also seeing into the living room and dining room. I can see Mark as he comes through the dining room with my leash in his hand. As soon as I see him, I get very excited and move to the front door, where he attaches the leash to my harness, opens the door, and lets me walk down the steps. As soon as he locks the door, off we go on our morning walk. In the wintertime, when the days are short, I find Mark around 4 p.m. in the living room, and I put my paw on his knee repeatedly, if necessary, to get him up and take me for a short walk. When we get back, he prepares my supper, which I eat around 5 p.m., go to the front porch and watch cars or bark at passersby, and go to bed between 5:30 and 6 p.m.

One time Mark told me: "I discover a sense of oneness between us, Shelbydog. It is like we are in sync. You can read my mind, and you can tell me what you want. You know by the way I walk when I am going outside, even before I invite you to come with me." As I listened to what he said, I agreed. I was thriving on a schedule that changed little from day to day. I knew our walking routes for morning, afternoon, and evening. There was a unity to our walking together, and there was a mutual consciousness between us. I was on a schedule for eating three meals a day, morning, noon, and evening. This unity was so pronounced that sometimes I just wanted to play with Mark. I would give the sign by hunkering down with my front paws and head. He would approach me, and I would run up and down the driveway, hiding behind bushes, running around the front of the house, hiding behind a tree, and running back to the front door. Inside the house, I would pick up a toy and run from the back steps through the dining room and living room and to the front porch. Sometimes I'd circle around, and Mark would follow me. Once I lay down on a rug, he would kneel beside me, and I'd roll on my side for a belly rub.

When it is cloudy and the sun doesn't shine through the front glass door, I am sad. And when I am sad, I am restless and bored or sleeping in my bed. If Mark is working outside, I go out with him and lie on the grass, where I can see the traffic on the streets. I love going for a ride in Mark's Jeep. He says, "Shelbydog, do you want to go for a ride?" and I come running through the house to get into the backseat of the Jeep. I remember one time when he was just backing the Jeep out of the garage to clean the garage, and I insisted on getting in. Even after he backed out the Jeep into the driveway and opened the backdoor for me to jump out, I stayed in it for a long time. When there is no sunshine the day before, I don't sleep well the following night. I get up two or three times and go to the rug in our bedroom to stretch; I can't stretch on the tile floors because my feet slide out from under me. Then, I go sit in my bed and awaken Mark with my paw on the edge of his bed. He leans over and pets me.

Some days when Mark is tired, we take a nap in the afternoon. He calls me, "Shelbydog, do you want to take a nap?" I go to my bed, and he lies on his bed. He may sleep for thirty minutes, and I may sleep for an hour or more. After he falls asleep and I don't, I get up and go back to my room, the front porch.

In early January 2020, while Corbin and Dani were living about fifty miles away, Mark told me: "Shelbydog, last night I watched you sleep on your afghan and pillow on the living room floor. You curled into a ball on your left side with your front paws over your back paws. Sometimes you breathed heavily; other times you breathed silently. At one point you barked softly and moved your paws as if you were running. I think you were dreaming." I don't fall asleep often in the living room; when I am tired, I go to my bed and go to sleep. I love being covered with my blanket, into which I bury my nose because it gets cold!

While taking our after-lunch, two-mile walk one day that same month, I walked by a dog almost exactly my color. The other dog was a little darker brindle with more red. The other dog stopped as did I, and we just looked at each other. Neither of us growled or barked. I think it was like looking into a mirror. I saw myself in the other dog, and he saw himself in me. That dog was the closest in color to me that I have ever seen.

Mark had given me only one bath, and that was after I had rolled in some poop in the backyard. When I went home for a day or two with Corbin and Dani, they gave me a bath every two or three weeks. By mid-January 2020, I really needed a bath, and there was little prospect that Corbin would take me home to get one in the upcoming weeks. So, Mark decided to give me a bath. He called me to my favorite rug and removed my bandana and harness. Then, he called me to follow him to the bathroom door, where he lifted me, took me into the bathroom, and set me in the shower, kicking shut the door while he did so. He wetted me with the shower nozzle, and I tried to get away; he held me in place. Then, using strawberry-scented body wash, he soaped me from nose to tail. I stood still in the shower, as he said to me: "What a good dog you are. I am not going to hurt you." After he rinsed the soap off me, he told me to step out of the shower and onto the bathroom rug, and I did. Then, taking a large towel, he dried me. I wiggled a lot and started to run away, but he kept calling me back, and he dried me from nose to tail. Finally, we finished. I was so happy that I ran through the house wanting to play. Mark came after me, saying, "Shelbydog smells so good now!" And I just smiled.

Playing took center stage when the weather turned very cold that January. Even after walking two miles, I wanted to play when we got back to the house. I'd hunker with my front paws and head on the ground and my butt in the air after Mark took off my leash. He'd take a step forward, saying, "I'm going to get that Shelbydog," and I'd run around the front yard, over the driveway, and hide behind the trash cart. Mark would start to move toward me, and I'd run down the driveway, across the front yard, and hide behind the bushes, waiting for him to find me. He'd approach saying, "I'm going to find Shelbydog," and I'd run by him. Once I tired, I'd lie on the grass and wait for him to open the door.

In late January 2020, we—Mark and I—had a visitor in the guest room for five days. I really like Matthew, our guest, so in the morning I would sit on the rug in the kitchen and wait for him to walk up the steps from the basement guestroom. If we had already taken our morning walk, I'd go to him, usually seated at the dining room table, as soon as Mark let me into the house. I like Matthew because he talks to me, pets me, gives me belly rubs, and treats me with respect. I even let him walk me; that is something I will not let everyone do. If I don't like someone, I will not move even though he or she has my leash in hand.

Even though Corbin was visiting me in Mark's house about once a week, he was not able to take me home with him too often. But when he did, I always enjoyed sitting in the chairs and sleeping on his and Dani's bed. When he brought me back to Mark's house, the first thing I did was jump on the love seat or on Mark's bed or the beds in the guest room. Mark would shout, "Shelby, get off that chair, love seat, bed." And I would jump down. Mark preferred that I lie on the rugs he gave me throughout the house, and that I sleep in my own bed. In other words, the license to be on the furniture that Corbin gave me was taken away by Mark. It wasn't all that bad, however, as I had a bed—something I didn't have at Corbin and Dani's house—and a pallet on the front porch, and rugs all through the house.

In early February 2020, there were many days without sunshine, and days without sunshine make me very restless. I leave the front porch and walk through the house to find Mark and get petted. On days without sunshine, I'm always ready to get my harness put on and go to the door, saying to Mark, "I'm ready to go." After talking to Matthew in 2022, Mark learned about the lamp therapy used by people who have SAD, seasonal affective disorder, a type of depression that is related to longer nights and shorter days. Mark wondered if it might work for me. He bought a sun lamp for me, and placed it on the front porch above the spot where I lie on the rug in front of the door. I love it. The brightness of the light is like being in sunshine without the accompanying warmth. That sun lamp is one of my prized possessions. On cloudy days Mark turns it on and I lie under it, pretending that I am soaking up rays of sunshine.

"I do not have the words to describe how much I love you, Shelbydog," I overheard Mark reading from the journal he keeps. "I tell you I love you several times a day, especially when I tuck you into your bed at night, pray with you, kiss you on the head, and pull your blanket over you. Within a few minutes you are sound asleep. I cannot imagine what my life was before you came to live here, and I cannot imagine what it would be like without you. I tell you I love you as soon as you get up in the morning and I put your harness and bandana on you." I don't think I was supposed to hear all that, but I was standing by the door, and he didn't see me there.

In early February 2020, Mark decided to give me a bath; that was my third bath from him. I had been scratching a lot and dragging my butt across the floor. I was in my bed when he got everything ready—assembling body wash, rugs, and towels in the bathroom. He tried calling me to come, but I knew what was about to take place; so I stayed in my bed. He came into the room and took off my bandana and harness and attempted to lift me, but I made myself as heavy as possible, and he couldn't pick me up! He tried again, and I went limp. Then, he pushed me onto a rug upon which he intended to pull me into the bathroom, but I would scoot back into my bed. Finally, he just pulled the bed and me over the tile floor and into the bathroom. I got up, but he shepherded me into the shower, where he wetted, shampooed, rinsed, and dried me. He kept saying, "You smell so good." I have to admit that I did smell good, and I was happy to be clean.

However, that afternoon in between rain showers, Mark took me to the backyard so I could pee. When I did not return in the allotted time, he came looking for me. He found me digging in a hole he had filled in. "Stop!" he shouted. "I told you not to dig there, didn't I?" he asked. I hung my head low. I hate being criticized. Then, I began to rub against Mark's leg to demonstrate how sorry I was. He walked into the garage, and I followed. I jumped on the bench so he could wipe away the mud on my paws before entering the house. I kept my head down, as I followed him into the living room and lay by his chair. He said, "I'm really disappointed that you dug that hole again after just getting a bath." I kept my head down and didn't move. After about thirty minutes, he bent down and began to pet me. I cannot tell you how great that felt! I rolled over and he scratched my belly. He said, "I'm sorry for being upset with you." As far as I was concerned that meant we were good again. To demonstrate my sincere sorrow, I spent most of that evening sleeping on my afghan near him in the living room. And I never dug in the backyard again.

In mid-February of 2020, I got invited with Mark to go to Barbara's house for drinks and cheese and crackers. I liked going to Barbara's house. I had been there for Thanksgiving 2019. This time Mark told me, "You have been the perfect house guest." I listened, got a few bites of cheese to eat, got a few crackers, drank water from Barbara's glass bowl, and fell asleep on her rug in front of the fire in her fireplace in the living room. Because I liked being where the action was, even though I fell asleep, I took the opportunity to do the same thing in Mark's house. When I lie on my afghan, Mark pets me and scratches my belly and gently rubs his hand over my side until I fall asleep. Then, he covers me with a blanket. I feel secure and loved when he treats me that way.

However, I also had my stubborn days. Being stubborn is what enabled me to survive the first five years of my life. Mark associated my stubbornness with the lack of sunshine. When we go for a walk, if I am in a stubborn mood, I do not want to go where Mark wants to take me. I pull and pull against the leash in an attempt to investigate a side street, and I find many ways to delay getting home. Once inside the house, I do not do what I am told. I will not let Mark put on my coat to protect me from the cold outside. On a stubborn day, I might get up at 8 a.m., go to the front door to see what is happening outside, and if it is dark and/or rainy, trot back to bed until 10 a.m. or 11 a.m. If the sun is shining, however, I am ready to go for a walk as soon as Mark is, and I look forward to the two-mile, post-lunch walk.

By the end of February 2020, those two-mile walks were leaving me rather stiff the next morning. I lumbered down the steps, wobbled on the sidewalks, and, when we got home, ate breakfast and went back to bed for most of the morning. After lunch, I walked very slowly before it rained. Then, I napped in the afternoon, ate my supper, and went to bed at 5 p.m. I slept all night. Mark was beginning to figure out that my body could not continue the two-mile walks. They were taking a toll on me. The day after, I wasn't limping or lumbering because I had gotten enough rest. I know Mark was worried about me, but my happiness that morning told him that I was feeling much better. I heard him praying and saying, "Thank you, God, for healing your servant, Shelbydog!"

8

MARK'S DOG

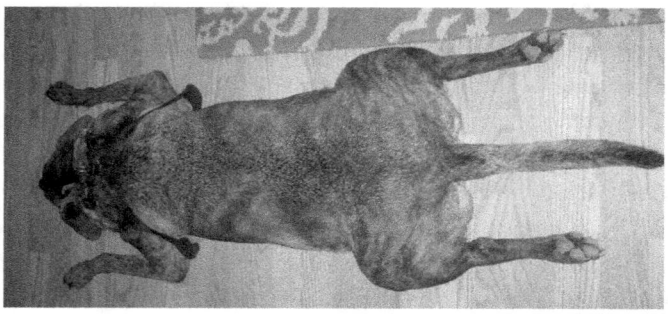

In late February 2020, Corbin was at Mark's house for dinner one night. And while they were eating and I was lying on my rug between the dining room and living room and listening to them, I heard Corbin tell Mark: "Dani has accepted the job offer made by her mother in Florida. And we are moving there in a few months. I guess that we will be taking Shelby with us." I was shocked, and I could tell Mark was too. I knew they were moving to Florida at the end of May, but they were coming back in July for some reason and to take me back with them before Mark left for his annual trip to Colorado. Ultimately, Mark cancelled the trip to Colorado due to the coronavirus pandemic that was spreading around the world. Both Mark and I began to grieve our separation, however. I began to think about all that he had taught me and shared with me. He told me: "When Matthew was here in January, he asked me what I had done to you, because you were such a different dog than the year before. I told him that I had decided to love you. And now you will be leaving me." While talking to me, Mark was holding me and hugging me.

I had heard Mark telling Matthew that he thought I was a universalizer, one who saw the big picture of the world, just like Mark, Matthew, and Corbin do. For Mark that explained why Corbin chose me in the shelter. I remember Mark saying to Matthew: "Shelby's world is so big that no kennel can contain her. She chooses to whom—people and other dogs—to relate. She chose you when you were here by gluing herself to you. Gradually, she chose Jared, our mail carrier. When she is with a few people, she chooses from among them who she wants to know; then, she goes to them repeatedly, leaving others alone. At a recent luncheon here, she chose one lady, who was not interested in relating to her, so she went to two people she knew. She chose me the first time she came here by listening to me and obeying me."

Mark continued: "Shelbydog is very smart. She knows where every cat, dog, and person she likes lives in the neighborhood, house by house. Her universalism is manifest in her deep sense of smell. Her leash is never long enough! She stands twitching her nose and absorbing every smell, then attempting to investigate its source. She wants to enter every open car, truck, and garage. Her superior sense of smell leads her to experience her world in depth. Her superior sense of hearing leads her toward whatever noises she hears." I listened attentively to what Mark was saying to Matthew. He really did know me.

"She always wants to walk farther, even when she is tired," Mark continued. "She often chooses where to walk, what route to take. She stops at street intersections and pans the area with her big brown eyes to see what is happening. She is like a queen surveying her kingdom. She keeps learning new words; she has the vocabulary of a six-year-old child. And she tries very hard to communicate. Sometimes she refuses to eat until she gets what she wants. I have taught her several new things, showing her only once or twice before she gets it. She is very comfortable going to her bed and sleeping in the room without me. She has grown in self-security and social skills while being with me for almost two years. She carries the presence of God with her; she is like the fire in the bush that doesn't burn but is overflowing with spirit."

That evening I remember Mark telling Corbin: "If you take her with you to Florida, your job is to continue to nourish all the growth that has taken place in her. I've learned that she thrives on a schedule of walking, eating, and sleeping. It gives her a sense of control over her life. She is no longer afraid of vacuum cleaners, sticks (brooms, mops, hoes, shovels, etc.), and men in work boots. She is precious to me. I've fallen in love with her and she with me. I once told you one time when you left her with me and your asked me how I was going to handle her, I said, 'I am going to love her,' and I have. She has taught me that she is not a dumb dog. She awakened compassion within me, and she interrupted my scheduled life to teach me to attend to her needs, even if they be only a pet or kiss on the head. Shelbydog and I have become friends with great respect for each other. She is at home here, and I am at home with her."

Mark continued telling Corbin: "She is your dog. I'm not going to let her divide us. If something doesn't work out in Florida, I'll take her back, no questions asked. I don't want you ever to think of putting her in a kennel or shelter. She is a free spirit, just like us. And she needs to be free to thrive. Furthermore, when you move, she has a bed, bandanas, and other things that need to be taken with her; they will help her feel at home in her new place to live. She needs to be walked two or three times a day. She needs to be fed three times a day. She gets tired faster as she gets older. She needs her own space, bed, rugs, food and water bowls, and toys to thrive."

By the end of February, it looked like I was going to Florida in a few months. In the meantime, I had decided to spend quality time with Mark. I had developed a morning ritual with him. After I got up, I'd stretch out on my bed, walk to the rug by Mark's bed, and stretch out again. Then, I'd walk through Mark's office, where he was, and he'd say, "Good morning, Madam Shelbydog!" I might turn my head and look at him! Through the dining room and into the living room I'd continue. On the big rug in the living room, I'd lie on my back and wiggle and wiggle and roll from side to side. Then, I'd stand up, shake, and stretch again before heading to the front porch to check the weather, maybe sitting in front of the door for a short time to observe it carefully. Then, I would get up and go find Mark. I would put my paw on his knee, telling him, "I'm ready for my morning walk."

I also had a ritual for my afternoon walk. After eating lunch at noon, Mark would go back to work in his office until around 2 p.m. Then, we would begin our two-mile walk with stops for me to rest and drink some water that Mark carried. Somedays he chose the route, and other days I chose the route we would go. One day in late February we were on our way out the front door, and I spotted a dog I had never seen in the next-door neighbor's yard. I headed over to the fence, where that dog came, and we smelled each other. I jumped on the fence, indicating that I wanted to play. So, Mark opened the gate and let me in. The two of us—dogs—ran around the yard and played and played. I was very happy, but I was also very tired. So, instead of walking two miles that day we walked only one.

I also have a funny story to tell about March 1, 2020. I went to bed around 6:30 p.m., and Mark came to the bedroom and pulled my blanket over me. He went to his office to work on a book he was writing. Then, two hours later he went to the living room to watch TV before going to bed. The door from the living room onto the front porch, my room, was still open; so, he shut the door and locked it. He heard some soft growling, but thought it was his stomach. After turning off the TV, he read for a while and heard more growling. So, he got up and opened the door to see from where the growling was coming. When he opened the door, I came in. After he had put me to bed, I got up and went back to my room unknown to him. When he shut the door, he presumed that I was sound asleep in the bedroom. He took me to the backyard so I could pee, and then both of us went to bed.

Mark and I are companions; literally, I know the word means to share bread. We share a house, a car, a bedroom, a bathroom, a yard, and more. We share walks, eating, sleeping, and more. I go with Mark on errands. I check on him several times a day, and he checks on me. When he goes outside, I accompany him. We are most companions when I spend time with him in the living room; we gaze into each other's eyes—contemplation, I think, it is called—and behold the divine presence nose to nose and loving each other deeply. We are companions on the journey of life. Both of us are making the most of the few months of travel that we have left together before I'm taken to Florida.

Thinking about leaving Mark and going to Florida made me very moody in early March. One day I would not do anything Mark told me to do: I wouldn't eat, get a drink, come when called, or even stay on the same side of the street when we were walking. The next day I would act more like Mark's companion: I'd eat my food, get a drink, come when called, and not attempt to keep crossing the street on walks. The next day I might be even more cooperative, especially if Corbin and Dani came to see me. "Dogs bring out the good in us," I heard someone say on TV. Mark said to me, "Shelby, that is exactly what you have done for me. You have brought out compassion and love." When he comes to the front porch to check on me, I roll over so he can rub my belly; that is what is important to me. I know he loves me. At night, when I awaken him to get petted and to pull my blanket over me, I just want to be acknowledged and loved.

One of my favorite places to ride to is the computer repair shop. Mark had some computer issues. Hal, the guy who runs the shop, has welcomed me to his place. He talks to me and pets me. In his first shop—from which he moved—I was able to sit at the door and watch the traffic on the street. Once I got bored, I walked around the shop, smelling all the computers and pieces on the floor. I was very well behaved there, and I continued that good behavior when I got home. I answered Mark's calls, ate my food, drank water, went for walks, and went to bed.

In mid-March 2020, Mark and I were still walking two miles after lunch. Often, on the weekends we would stop at Barbara's house. Barbara would give me a glass bowl of water; after a few times, I expected to get a glass bowl of water! Just like I expected to get three crackers handed to me by Barbara. I remember one time when Barbara attempted to give me the crackers by leaving them in the foil holder. I wouldn't eat them until she handed them to me! After that walk Mark became more aware that a two-mile walk was best for me only a few times a week because it really makes me tired. And it didn't take long for him to change that to only a mile on most days, while reserving two miles for Sundays. I can remember when I could walk five miles, but my age is catching up to me. Now, we walk about a half a mile in the morning, a mile after lunch, and a half a mile before or after supper. And that is enough.

When I am tired, I want to be petted and have my belly scratched. I like finding Mark in the house and putting my paw on his knee no matter what he may be doing. He knows that I want attention, and he gives it to me. As a treat for him, I will fall asleep in the evening by his chair in the living room, while he is watching TV and after I get pampered with petting and belly rubs. I fall into deep sleep and snore after Mark covers me with a blanket. I look so peaceful and innocent and depend upon him to take care of me that it can bring tears to his eyes. One evening I had a terrible itch on my hip, and so I scratched it. Mark examined me and found a pimple. After he put some antibiotic ointment on it, it stopped irritating me. He said to me: "You evoke so much love and divine presence that I am overwhelmed by emotion. I feel deep compassion, deep peace, deep humility that I get to share such moments with you. I don't feel worthy to be in your divine presence. Thank you for this special time." Then, he kissed me.

The next Sunday after he petted me and scratched my belly, I lay on the big rug in the living room, and I listened to what Mark said: "I love these moments of beholding each other. Not only do I behold you, but you behold me. It is an experience of being emptied and filled simultaneously. Your emptying leads me to recognize the divine in you, and my emptying leads you to recognize the divine in me. And all we can do is behold the divine presence in each other." I think he was right, except when he decides to give me a bath. Then, all I behold is the walk-in shower in front of me, and I refuse to walk into it! I may come into the bathroom, but I lie down in front of the shower. Mark picks up my front feet and puts them in the shower, then he picks up my back feet and scoots all of me into the shower. I can be a little more cooperative because I know what is going to happen next. He doesn't hurt me as he gets me wet, puts shampoo on me, rubs it into my fur and all over my body, and talks to me all the time, saying: "Be still! Stop wiggling! No shaking! Be a good girl!" Then, he rinses off the soap, tells me to stand still for a minute while all the water drains off me, wraps me in a towel, and helps me step out of the shower. He rubs the towel all over me to dry my fur, even the fur between my toes! Then, he opens the bathroom door and lets me out. I run through the house to the front porch in joy.

In mid-March 2020, Mark said something that got me thinking. "I am amazed how aware you are of your size," he stated. He was, of course, accurate. I instinctively knew how much a door needed to be opened in order for me to pass through it. I knew how much room I needed to get around furniture, like behind chairs or between things, without getting stuck. I would not force myself into small spaces. I knew it demonstrated by self-awareness, my ability to reflect on myself and my size. One morning, this led Mark to talk to me on our walk. He said to me: "Being with you, Shelbydog, has turned me into a Shelbydogologist, one who knows all about Shelbydogs! The study of Shelbydogs is Shelbydogology. Anyone who is too focused on Shelbydogs suffers from Shelbydogism, for which there is no known cure." Mark laughed, and I laughed with him.

All seriousness aside, even in late March 2020 I was still suffering from fear of thunder and lightning. I remember being awakened one morning round 5:30 a.m. Mark was already up and sitting in his office reading. I went and sat on the rug near him; he petted my head. When the thunder stopped, I went back to bed, but when it began again, I went back to him. We couldn't go for a walk because of the rain, but he needed me to go outside and pee before he left for a doctor's appointment. Because I would not leave the house if I felt a raindrop on my head, he put on my coat when it was just sprinkling. That was enough to get me to walk out into the backyard and pee. When he returned about an hour later, I gave him a hearty reception, but we still had to wait to go on a walk. Mark fed me, and I went back to bed and fell asleep. Around 10 a.m. he awakened me to go on a walk. After lunch we were able to walk again, and, after we got home, I went to bed for a nap.

At night I often got up and went to the kitchen, where my water bowl was, to get a drink. I was warm. When I came back to the bedroom, I lay on my bed, but it was too hot, so I got up and lay on the tile floor, where it was cool, and I slept there for a few hours. It was getting warmer and warmer in the house, and Mark had not yet begun to turn on the window air conditioner in our bedroom. I was getting very hot in the sun during our after-lunch walk, even though Mark carried a bottle of water and gave me frequent drinks of it in his left hand. By the time we got back, my tongue was hanging out of my mouth, and I would find a cool area of tile and lay spread eagle on it to cool off. I even learned where all the air conditioning vents were in the house: one in the kitchen, one in the dining room, and two in the living room. I would stretch out in front of them to cool.

One afternoon, while I was cooling, Mark sat on the floor by me and said: "I wonder how you see the day ahead of you in the morning?" I thought that was a good question. I thrive on a set schedule, and I know that such a schedule exists. I don't rely upon Mark to activate my day; I rely upon him to walk me and feed me. I do know when some things should happen, like when it is time to walk, to eat, to pee, or to poop. In fact, Mark often says to me, "Shelby, let's go outside and go pee-pee." And he opens the backdoor, we go outside, and I go to my favorite place in the grass to pee.

As I digested the experience of getting a bath from Mark, I was getting more and more cooperative every time he gave one to me. One day in late March, after a FedEx truck delivered some new canned dog food and a new harness, Mark gave me a taste of the turkey and chicken grill in a little bowl because I had not eaten my breakfast that morning. I liked the new food. He put more of it on the food in my bowl, and I licked the bowl clean. Then, he called me to the bathroom. I went and lay in front of the shower. He pushed me in, bathed me, and dried me with a fluffy towel. Then, he opened my new harness and began adjusting it to fit me. After our post-lunch walk, he adjusted it more. I got a new harness because he had to repair my old one. Some of the protective covering under my front legs was coming loose. The next day, which I will never forget, we went to the backyard, where the dwarf red bud tree was blooming profusely and billions of bees were buzzing around its blossoms. I attempted to catch the bees in my mouth as I jumped up and down. Mark could hear my teeth clicking together as I attempted to catch a bee. Not a one did I manage to get! Mark said to me: "The burning bush Shelbydog is trying to catch bees on the burning bush red bud tree. So much of divinity is overwhelming."

In early April 2020, spring was well underway, and after Mark mowed the yard, he would let me out of the house unleashed to lie in the yard in the sun, while he weeded the flower gardens. When I got hot, I moved to the shade to cool, then back to the sun, then back to the shade. After getting tired, I would sit in front of the door from the garage into the house. Mark knew that meant, "I want to go inside," and he would open the door and let me in.

I also began to change the order of eating my food. Mark had been giving me my kibble, then my dental bone, then my piece of tracheae, then a milk bone or two. I decided that I wanted my piece of tracheae first, then my dental bone, then a few bites from Mark's plate, then my milk bone. Likewise, when it came to breakfast, I wanted something from Mark's plate, even though he had been up a long time before me and already eaten his breakfast. One morning to satisfy me, he found a couple of bites of leftover pasta in the refrigerator and put that on my food. That was exactly what I wanted, and he figure it out.

For some reason from time to time, I would get very nervous, like sitting in the veterinarian's examination room. When I got nervous, tremors occurred in my front legs, and I would shake. When Mark was near me, he would hold me close to himself and rub my legs until the tremors stopped. The only time that still occurs is when I am taken to the vet.

In mid-April, a large load of free mulch from All About Trees was dumped in our driveway. While Mark shoveled mulch into a wheelbarrow and hauled it all around the house, our next-door neighbor did the same, and I got to be outside with them unleashed. After spending a few days outside watching them work, and sneaking to the mulch to roll and roll in it, I was tired and slept a lot once I got back into the house. Then, the temperature cooled, and I was full of energy, walking and running.

I think Mark figured out my tail wagging. When I hear him walking through the house to our bedroom, the living room, or the front porch, I cannot help but wag my tail because someone I love is approaching me.

When he starts talking to me, my tail takes off. When I've gotten into trouble with Mark, my tail hangs down very low. I communicate a lot with my tail. However, even though I cannot speak, I know a lot of words, like drink, ride, good, coat, hurry-hurry, walk, blanket, food, bed, nap, wait, bone, NOW, stop, no, outside, bath, harness, water, sit, slowly, pool, pretty, treat, bone, and more.

Over the three-years that I had been with Mark, I had been aging and slowing down. When I was six years old, we would often walk five miles together. When I was seven years old, it started to become difficult for me to walk two miles at the same time. By the time I was eight, even one mile, when it was hot, wore me out. Mark had to coax me to finish the last half a mile. We still try to walk two miles on the weekend, but we have to stop for water and rest two or three times. I was also sleeping more, usually getting twelve hours of sleep a night, and in the winter, I often slept thirteen to fifteen hours. Mark, of course, observed me slowing. So, in light of that observation, he changed our schedule to walking a mile in the morning, while it was still cool, and maybe another mile after supper, depending on how hot it was.

Near the end of April I got to watch Barbara's son and grandsons dismantle her back porch-deck in preparation for the installation of a new one. I lay on the cool concrete driveway and watched intently as the father and sons took the old porch-deck apart piece by piece. Once we left there, we met Jared, the mail carrier, on the way home. He was sitting in his truck, taking a break. I went over to him, he talked to me, and petted me, while I nosed around his mail truck. As he got out of the truck, I took my play position, which he recognized. Then, we ran around each other for a few minutes. I had a good time playing with Jared.

Four days later, we came across Jared again. When we got to his truck, he got out after petting me and talking to me. I hunkered down in the play position tempting him to play with me as he did before. He played with me for a short time because he needed to get back to work delivering the mail. On another day, while walking on the sidewalk, I could hear Jared talking on the phone, but I could not see him. I would stop and turn my head, listening to his voice. Then, I would walk a few feet and stop and turn my head listening to him, but still I couldn't see him. Finally, I turned around and saw him. I pulled the leash with Mark on the other end toward him. Mark turned me lose so I could run to Jared to play. Indeed, once I knew his smell, we would stop by his parked truck and I would smell the door and know it was Jared, my friend.

On our walks, I have also discovered a way to slow down and cool. I come to an abrupt stop when I see tall grass and I throw myself onto it and roll over and over, laughing all the while. Not only is the grass cool as I roll, but it gives me (and Mark) a short rest during our walk. When I am outside on the driveway, I like to try to catch bees visiting the blooming plants growing there. Mark says to me, "Shelbydog, leave those bees alone." And I go and lie down until he cannot see me anymore, and I go back to try to catch a bee.

Mark filled my pool. On this hot early May day, while he was working outside, I took dips in the pool three times to cool. When we finally decided to go inside, I remembered to jump onto the bench so Mark could dry me with a towel before I got back in the house. While I'm happy sitting in the water over my back, I'm happier when Mark is rubbing me dry with a towel and talking to me.

By the time I reached my eighth year of life, I was not able to continue to walk two miles at any given time, even if the temperature was cool or mild. I just got tired. So, because I got tired so fast and my tongue hanged out of my mouth and I slowed down by rolling in the grass, Mark had to change our daily routine. We began to walk a mile in the cool of the morning. Then, if it were still cool, we would walk a mile after lunch. Once it got hot outside, we might walk a mile after supper or just around the block, depending on the degree of the humidity.

9

SICK DOG

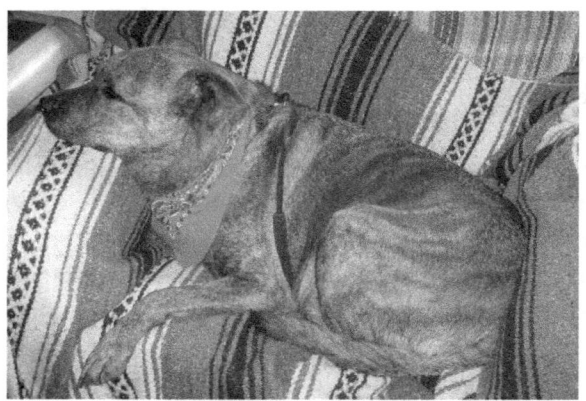

In mid-May 2020, during my eighth year of life, I was outside in the back-yard with Mark one Sunday afternoon. While he planted some seeds in the potting shed and repotted some plants, I got in and out of my pool. Unknown to Mark, I had an upset stomach and ate what I thought was grass but was daylily leaves. Around 4 p.m. that afternoon, while Mark was reading in the living room and I was resting on the front porch, I made my way into the living room retching a little on the door frame and rug. Mark got up immediately to see what was the matter with me, but I returned to the front porch. After he cleaned up the mess I had just made, he came to the front porch where he found a pile of vomit consisting of daylily leaves and bile. He cleaned up that mess, too. He petted me and kept asking me,

"Are you OK?" I must have been because I ate my dinner about an hour later and even went on a short evening walk.

The next day, Monday, after a good night's sleep, I felt better, but I was still not feeling like my usual self. Mark put out my usual and favorite foods for dinner, and I only nibbled on them. He tried everything in his dog pantry. Finally, I became very hungry and ate a little of what was in my bowl or on the rug by it. On Tuesday, we went on our morning walk, but I would not eat anything after we returned. Again, Mark was so concerned that he got out all kinds of things from his dog pantry—chicken, turkey, dental bone, trachea, cheese, canned food, and more, but I would not eat anything. He cooked rice for me that afternoon and put some chicken noodle soup on it, but I wouldn't eat it. He coached me to eat some for dinner, along with my regular kibble—lamb and rice—a dental bone and some other small bones. I also found a rawhide chip to chew on.

Mark said to me: "Why are you not eating? Was it Saturday's daylily leaves? Sunday's flea and tick medicine? Sunday's heart worm medicine? Allergies, depression because of no sun for several days, something else?" I could tell that he was very worried about me. "I see you lose strength all day long when you don't eat, and that bothers me very much. I feel helpless as to what I need to do." On Wednesday evening, after a full day, I threw up my breakfast, lunch, and dinner. Then, I was very restless during the night with labored breathing. On Thursday morning, I went on my morning walk, peed, pooped, but would not eat anything nor drink any water. Mark called my vet, who told him to drop me off at the clinic as soon as possible, and I would be worked in to the vet's full schedule. He got me there at 9 a.m. and came and got me at 12:45 p.m. I underwent a bevy of tests, while becoming very nervous.

Before I was brought to him after he arrived at the clinic, the vet told him that I had not absorbed any toxicity from the daylily leaves. "She has a very upset stomach," said Heidi, my vet. Heidi gave Mark some anti-nausea medicine to help settle my tummy along with some easily digestible dog food. After Mark told her about my allergies, she told him to give me one and a half Claritin tablets. Then, the vet's assistant brought me from the back of the clinic. And when she opened the door, I saw Mark standing there, and I pulled the leash out of the assistant's hand and ran to him. He knelt down and petted me, while I licked him and jumped in joy to see him. Then, he led me to the Jeep, into which I jumped, and he took me home.

He gave me the anti-nausea medicine and half a can of the easily digestible dog food. Later, we went for a short walk, came home, and I rested, taking a nap for most of the afternoon. For dinner, Mark mixed the soft dog food with some cooked rice, which I ate. However, I was very tired, sad, and slow. I didn't feel good because of the medicine. However, day by day I got better as I took my medicine for three days and ate the easily-digestible turkey and chicken canned food. Mark began to give me a little of my usual food until I was totally on my own diet. The Claritin was helping a lot, reducing my snoring and clearing my clogged nose. I was sleeping soundly. Mark had me back to my usual breakfast and dinner feedings. And our new walking schedule—a mile in the morning, a short walk after lunch, and a short walk after dinner—was firmly in place.

I became sad when Corbin and Dani stopped by to see me on their move to Florida. However, my sadness quickly turned to happiness, as I realized that I would not be moving again. I was settled with Mark and at home. I was feeling better, eating my food, and relaxing. I knew where my things—bed, toys, rugs, pool, bowls—were, and I was home for the first time in my life.

On May 31, 2020, Mark took me on a mile morning walk. I peed and pooped and even ran a little in the cool air. But when we got back home and he fixed my breakfast, I would not eat. He tried several things, but nothing could coax me into eating my food. Around 11 a.m. he gave me two Pepto Bismol tablets, and twenty minutes later I ate some food. He figured out that my stomach was upset again, and the Pepto Bismol settled it. I ate three crackers and drank water from a glass bowl at Barbara's that afternoon. Before dinner, Mark gave me two more Pepto Bismol tablets, and I ate the supper he had prepared for me. After a short walk, I went to bed around 7:45 p.m. The next day, June 1, 2020, he had to give me two more Pepto Bismol tablets after our morning walk in order to get me to eat my breakfast. After that I was very lackadaisical for the rest of the morning. After lunch I walked a square block and headed back home.

Mark had called my vet at 7:30 a.m., but he didn't hear from her until 4:30 p.m. He explained to her what was happening to me, but she had no idea as to what might be wrong. He explained to the vet that I had eaten my supper, and it looked like I was feeling better. Mark mentioned the fatty trachea pieces might be the problem; he was going to withhold them from me for a few days to see if they were upsetting my stomach. The vet asked him to call her the next day and leave a report as to how well I was doing.

I ate all my food on June 2 because my stomach was settled. I ate all my food on June 3, but Mark told the vet, "The heat and humidity really affect Shelby. She doesn't like being out of the house except for a few minutes or a very short walk."

The next day, June 4, I ate all my food. That evening we went for a walk and ran across one of my dog friends, Ro, and his master, and Mark let us run and play in the front and back yard. I was very happy and excited, and I slept soundly that night. On June 5, Mark called and talked to the vet about me. He told Heidi that I was feeling better, eating my food, taking my medications, and being slowed down by the humidity. The vet told him that I could get no more trachea nor cheese nor anything else with fat in it. "Fat is upsetting her stomach," the vet told Mark. "She is one of those dogs who cannot tolerate fat." And that was the end of two of my favorite foods! Mark said to the vet, "I have Shelby back." I was eating my food and feeling a lot better. I even pestered Mark to take me for a long walk, making a stop at Barbara's for water in a glass bowl and three crackers. After we left there, I ran over Barbara's lawn because I felt so good.

During our morning walk on June 8, I began to limp a little, but walked it off in a few steps. The same thing occurred after lunch. We walked before dinner in order to avoid the coming rain, and I limped. Mark noticed. He told me, "I think it is a combination of heat, humidity, and maybe a little arthritis. I've made a note to talk to the vet about it." By the middle of June, I was feeling really good. I was excited and wanted to play. I liked stopping and rolling in the grass. I liked going to my pool to cool. I liked jumping on the bench in the garage so Mark could dry me. I was very playful, meeting Mark at the door with a rawhide bone and leading him to the front porch, where I'd lie for him to pet me. On our walks, I loved to break into a trot and run. I was feeling well and happy.

I went to the vet on June 21 to get my annual check-up and shots. When Mark escorted me into the examination room, I sat on the bench next to him. While he was answering the assistant's questions about me, I began to tremble, and Mark put his arm around me and held me tight to himself. He held me after the assistant finished and the vet came in. Then, I had to jump to the floor, so the vet could examine me and give me my shots and inject foul-tasting liquid into the corner of my mouth! Then, I was back on the bench with Mark's arm around me. After we got home, Mark said to me: "Your tremors indicate some bad experiences in veterinary offices, or they indicate your fear of something. I don't know which it is. When it thunders, you shake, but we have worked on that a lot so that your fear is diminished. All I can do is love you and work with you toward removing your fears as much as possible."

With my stomach settled, by the end of June, I was a very happy dog. On our morning walks, I would stop and roll and wiggle two or three times. I would trot on the sidewalk. I would cool in my pool. I would go to bed early, and get up the next day and be ready to do it all over again. One evening while Mark was playing with me on the floor, he noticed a raw spot under one of my front legs. It was caused by my pulling against the harness attached to the leash. Mark put Polysporin on it to heal it and Cortizone to stop the itching. Except for my stubborn streak and always wanting table food on my food, I was very happy.

In early July 2020, Mark began to suspect that my rolling in the grass might be due to a skin allergy. He had noticed when he petted me sometimes that I had withers, like a horse, especially on my back. So, he called my vet, who told him to give me Benadryl. My vet also told him that I needed to be on a flea and tick medicine; Corbin had told Mark that it was mixed with my heart worm medication, but that was not true. So, Mark got heart worm medication from the vet and Benadryl at the pharmacy. After a few days, the Benadryl had not stopped my itching and scratching. Corbin told Mark, "Shelby's itching and scratching is seasonal. I never did anything about it, and it went away on its own." Mark called the vet to report on the Benadryl's ineffectiveness and she prescribed Apoquel, a drug for dogs with skin allergy. Within two days, there was a change. My itching had abated, and the scratching had stopped. I felt so good that I wanted to play with Mark. I ran more. When Mark petted me, the withers had disappeared. We had passed another hurdle. Mark figured out that it was not my skin that was sensitive; it was the fact that I have allergies that affect my skin. Without the irritation to my skin, and without an upset stomach, I sometimes walked a mile in the evenings, even though it was hot.

Another significant change took place. When taking the Benadryl, I was not eating. When Mark gave me medications, he wrapped them in soft, canned dog food and put them in a small porcelain bowl. When I wasn't eating, he took my food out of the tin bowl I usually ate from and put them in a large porcelain bowl, and I ate it. Hereafter, Mark put my food in a large serving bowl; I liked the feel of that bowl on my tongue. I would lick the bowl all around the inside. When it cracked and broke, he bought me a heavy white serving bowl that would not scoot across the floor when I licked its sides. That became my permanent feeding bowl.

By mid-July I had a new friend, Conan, a white Labrador retriever, who lived only two houses away from me. He was a puppy, and he accepted me as the alpha female I am. When we met his owner walking him and Mark walking me, they took off our leashes and let us run and play and roll each other until we were so tired that we couldn't get up. If one of us could find a stick, each of us would take an end of it and chew on it until our owners recaptured us and continued our walks. Both of us wore happy faces when playing with each other. A few times a week we would meet Conan and his owner on our walk, and they would always let us play and run until we were tired.

Mark and I settled into our revised daily routine. After I awoke, he would put on my harness, then my bandana, attach my leash, and take me on a walk. After we returned home, he fixed my breakfast and fed me. Then, I would spend the rest of the morning on the front porch watching cars drive by and people walk or bicycle by on the streets. I might nap on my rug or pallet on the front porch, even softly growling at cats, dogs, people, and trucks. After eating my lunch, I liked to wait for Jared to bring the mail. Mark would open the door and let me go to the driveway to greet him, and he would play with me after I presented him my bone or one of my toys. He would always give it back, but he usually held it up high so I would jump trying to get it or toss it in the air to see if I could catch it. When I got tired of playing with Jared, I would walk back to the front porch. If it were cool outside, Mark would take me for an afternoon walk; if it were warm, we would wait until after dinner. I liked to eat around 5 p.m., go for a walk around 6:30 p.m., come back and rest, and go to bed around 7 p.m.

At any time during the day, I was ready to go with Mark on errands. He taught me the word *ride*. He'd say, "Shelby, do you want to go for a ride?" and I'd come running through the house to the door that opened into the garage. He'd open the back door of the Jeep, and I'd jump in. I'd go with him, even if his stops were places I couldn't go into. Within a year, I no longer needed to hear the word *ride*. I had learned to associate the sound of the keys on his ring jingling together with a ride. So, if I heard the jingling, I'd be headed for the Jeep.

One day in mid-July, Mark told me: "Shelby, we have grown very close to each other with a trust of each other than amazes me. You trust me when I put salve on your wounds, give you a bath, check you for ticks, examine you in general, cover you with your blanket, feed you, give you water, prepare your medicine, and on and on. There is a symbiosis that has developed between us, even to sleeping next to each other in our respective beds. And I am more and more comfortable around you. I trust you to come when I call, not to destroy anything in the house, not to run away when you are unleashed and outside, not to bite me when I examine you, and on and on." I will remember those words, because they meant so much to me. Truly, we had a special relationship, one that I had never had before.

One morning in late July, the humidity was high and I got very hot running and playing with Conan. Later in the morning while Mark was doing something with one of his friends on the driveway, I ate some grass to settle my upset stomach. Within a few minutes I had vomited the grass and some of my breakfast on the grass. This upset Mark. He gave me two Pepto Bismol tablets to settle my tummy. He also noticed that my skin sensitivity was back. So, he called my vet, who told him to put me back on Apoquel two times a day for a week and then one a day after that. Within a day I was feeling better. Mark determined that I would be taking Apoquel for the rest of my life, so he ordered it from Chewy at half the cost he was paying the vet. He told me: "The Apoquel controls your skin allergies and keeps you from scratching and biting yourself." He also put me back on Claritin to clear my nose and eyes. Now I take one Apoquel every day and Claritin during the spring, summer, and fall.

By mid-August 2020, the next issue Mark had to address with me had arisen. One night, I awakened him at 4:30 a.m. I wanted to go outside, indicated by sitting on the bedroom rug and looking toward the bedroom door. Mark understood what I needed to do. So, he took me to the backyard, where I went off and pooped. I had diarrhea. Later, on our morning walk, I had diarrhea again. When we got back, I ate my breakfast, but I didn't feel well, and Mark knew that. So, he gave me two doses of Pepto-Bismol, which made me feel better by the afternoon. I ate my dinner, and Mark took me for a short after-supper walk. The mornings were very cool, and I especially enjoyed meeting Conan and his owner, so Conan and I could play and run. By late August, the diarrhea was back. One morning Mark gave me three doses of two Pepto Bismol tables and fed me white rice. After more diarrhea that afternoon, he gave me another dose of medicine. Two days before that, Conan and I had played in two different yards along the sidewalk, where our paths had crossed. At first, Mark and Conan's owner didn't see that one yard was covered in dog poop. Mark concluded that I had gotten some of the poop on my feet, which I licked clean. Some bacteria or virus was in that poop, and that was what gave me diarrhea. For that day he fed me white rice to be sure that the diarrhea was arrested.

But it wasn't. The next evening's post-dinner walk featured more diarrhea. During the night, I awakened Mark because I needed to go outside Then, he called the vet, who put me on a twenty-four hour fast. I didn't like that at all. When the fast was over, I got very small increments of white rice with very few pieces of boiled chicken breast. The next day, all my meals were the same: rice and chicken. During the first week of September 2020, I had good days and bad days. The vet thought I might have parasites from the dog poop in which I had stepped, so Mark took a sample of my poop there to be examined. I had no parasites. Mark put me back on my regular diet. One night during that week, we had company for dinner. I found a rawhide bone and chewed on it for a long time. At 2:30 a.m. I awakened Mark with an upset stomach; he let me outside but could not see what I was doing in the dark. After coming in, he gave me a dose of Pepto Bismol. We went back to bed, but thirty minutes later I had to awaken him again. Before we could get outside, however, I threw up daylily leaves on the floor. He cleaned up the mess I had made, and he gave me another dose of Pepto Bismol. We went back to bed, but I needed to go outside again. So, at 4 a.m. Mark got up and stayed up. I lay by him in his office chair until the Pepto took effect; then I went back to my bed. I was back on white rice and boiled chicken! Mark was convinced that it was the rawhide bone that had upset my stomach. So, he gathered the one I had and any pieces I had broken off and threw all away. Over the next few days I began to feel better with no upset stomach, no diarrhea. Even the white rice and chicken began to taste good in my hunger. I was able to sleep later in the morning and enthusiastically to go on my morning walk. By evening, I was starving; Mark was gradually weaning me off the white rice and chicken and back onto my regular diet.

After all this, one evening Mark was watching TV and I was lying on the front porch. I began to bark and growl as if I were being attacked. Mark came to see what was the matter. He observed the direction I was looking and saw a hummingbird sipping nectar from a large blossom near the door. In the shadow of the dusk-to-dawn light, the hummingbird looked huge as it fluttered and created shadows that made it look like a hawk. I growled loudly. Mark put his arm around me, laughed, and said, "It' not going to hurt you." By then, it had flown away. Mark helped to settle me. "No huge bird is attacking you," he said.

Just when I and Mark think that we have me balanced, something else takes place! While a friend of ours was visiting and I was soliciting belly rubs, she found a bump on my breast bone. She showed Mark where it was, and he touched it, too. The next day he called the vet and got an appointment for me to see her that afternoon. As he walked me into the vet's office, I became very nervous, finding it impossible to sit on the bench near Mark and not walk around the small examination room. Mark had to wrestle me to get me on my back on the floor so the vet could examine the lump. The vet determined that it was a benign fatty lipoma. She told Mark to watch it and to let her know if it got bigger. As soon as the vet finished checking me, I was ready to leave. Mark took me to the Jeep, I jumped in, and we went home. Mark fed me, walked me, and calmed me. "I'm very relieved that you do not have a tumor or cancer," he told me.

In late September, I was spending a lot of time outside. While Mark worked in the garage building something over a few days, I was outside without a leash with him. I'd lie on the grass in the sun until I got too hot, then I'd move to the cool concrete of the driveway or the garage floor. I liked waiting for my friend, Jared, when he came to deliver mail in the afternoon. He always talked to me, played with me, and scratched my belly. The cooler the weather became, the happier I was. When not being outside, I enjoyed accompanying Mark on errands. "Do you want to go for a ride?" he'd ask. And I'd be ready to jump into the back seat of the Jeep. At some stops I got to go in, but at others I had to stay in the Jeep.

By early October, I was able to walk two-miles on a cool day. One day Mark walked me to a park. He was amazed how well I remembered the route and where we stopped so he could give me a drink of water. We had not taken that route for six months, but I knew the way. I have to admit that two miles made me very tired. So, that night I went to be bed at 7 p.m. In general, when I am tired, I go to bed. Mark sees me walk through the house to our bedroom. I step onto and lie on my bed. A few minutes after I get settled, he comes and pets me, prays with and for me, kisses me good night, and puts my blanket on me.

By mid-October, the cool weather had caused me to regrow my very fine under fur. I was very content and very centered living with Mark. His friends who visited him became my friends who also visited me. They brought me toys, bandanas, and other things, and I solicited belly scratches from them and licked their hands in gratitude. Two major incidences oc-curred during that time. The first was on a morning walk. I saw something in the back yard of a home we passed and suddenly jerked the leash Mark was holding. The jerk pulled him over and against a retaining wall. He scraped the knuckles on his left hand on the wall and his elbow on the pave-ment and his left knee on the sidewalk. When I turned and looked at him, he was bleeding in five places with blood oozing in several more. I thought we would turn around and go home, but we continued the mile walk. After we got home, I watched as he washed his wounds and put ointment on them. I kept my head down the rest of that day because I knew it was my sudden jerking of the leash that had caused him to fall.

A few days later the second incidence occurred. After supper, I, un-characteristically, wanted to go outside, and Mark took me to the backyard, where I pooped soft manure. I awakened him at 12:30 a.m. to go outside and poop again and at 5:15 a.m. Diarrhea was back with more pooping at 7 a.m. Mark fixed me white rice and boiled chicken for my meals that day. By the next day, I wasn't any better, having gotten Mark up three times the night before. He tried giving me Imodium AD during the night. While he was gone for a short time the next morning, I threw up the little food I had eaten and the Imodium AD with lots of bile. He cleaned up the mess and called the vet, who put me on another twenty-four-hour fast, followed by white rice and chicken. I was in recovery again.

After watching it rain most of one day in mid-October, Mark took me on a walk in mid-afternoon in between showers. He called me to come to the rug so he could get me ready. I brought him my bone, which I dropped on the rug by us. He picked up the bone and put it in my toy box. After he put on my harness, I picked up the bone from the box and put it back on the rug. Mark laughed, then we went for our walk. A few days after that funny incident, Mark brought me a bone after breakfast; I was on the front porch. I ate it and threw up all the food I had recently eaten. He cleaned up the mess, boiled chicken, and fixed white rice for me. I think he expected diarrhea, but that never happened. He told me, "I think you ate too fast, and that upsets your stomach." Nevertheless, I got two Pepto Bismol tablets and rice and chicken that day. In order to slow down my eating, Mark began giving me things in stages. He concluded that excitement hindered diges-tion for some reason. So, I get a little bit of food. Then, after a short while, I get a bone. Then, there is a pause before whatever is the next item in my diet. I eat my meals when he eats his meals. I have to come to him to get each item in my diet.

Near the end of October, I listened to Mark as I was falling asleep on my afghan in the living room. I had my head on my pillow, but before I started to snore, I heard him say, "Shelbydog, you are so sweet, and you have been so much fun today." He petted my side repeatedly and continued: "I love you so much. I thank God for you being in my life. You are the presence of God with me. It is a privilege to take care of you." Not only had I found a permanent home, but I had also found love, security, and protection.

10

DIET EVALUATION

THE NEXT PHASE OF my adjustment began on the last night of October 2020. I awakened Mark three times during the night to go outside; I had diarrhea again. After both of us got up and we went for a walk, I pooped a fourth time. Mark didn't need to call the vet to know what to do; I was back on white rice and boiled chicken. The next night I got him up one time, and I had diarrhea on our morning walk. When we got back, he called the vet for an appointment and a meeting with her in two days. I heard him tell her, "There is something else going on with Shelby, but I don't know what it is." I fasted for twenty-four hours. Then, the day of the appointment and meeting, I ate white rice and boiled chicken.

Before the day of the appointment and meeting, Mark made a list of everything I had been eating since I came to live with him. On the day of the appointment and meeting, the vet and Mark spent about thirty minutes going over the list and putting together a plan to eliminate the diarrhea that had been recurring in me. I listened as my vet told Mark that some of my food had too much fiber in it for me. They crossed off a number of items, including some kibble and canned food and other things. When they were finished, I had a diet of lamb and rice kibble, two canned foods of turkey and chicken in which my medicine could be wrapped, a dental bone, and two kinds of Milk Bones. Over the course of a few months, some of my favorite foods—rawhide bones, trachea pieces, salmon and rice canned food, etc.—had been removed from my diet. Mark was satisfied with the appointment and meeting, and I was, too. Just in case occasional diarrhea occurred, my vet gave Mark a prescription of Endosorb tablets, a dog's anti-diarrhea medication. During our afternoon walk that day, I found a pile of leaves, jumped in it, and rolled around. I was happy and funny. Mark laughed at me. The vet had given him the number of calories I needed every day, and that was now his guide for feeding me. He made a chart of what I got, how much I got, and what the calorie count was. I was on the way to dog wholeness!

The next day Mark spent part of it gathering the food I could no longer have. I watched him carry a bag and cans to the garage. A few days later, I went with him to the Humane Society, where he made a donation of the food to the shelter. I was feeling much better by November 5. On the morning of November 6, 2020, Conan stopped by my house to play with me. We ran through the front yard and over the driveway until I was tired and lay down. As I often did, I bent my front left paw under me. Conan, who had grown into a big, white Labrador jumped on me in play and sprained my foot. I squealed when he jumped on me. Then, I stood up, keeping my left paw off the ground. Conan's owner put his leash back on, and they went home. I limped up the front steps and lay on my pallet on the front porch. When I went into the house to eat or get a drink of water, I limped. Mark took me to the backyard so I could pee, but I limped.

In the afternoon, he took two strips of cloth and wrapped them tightly around my foot. It was like he put an ankle, knee, or elbow brace on me. The tightly-wound bandage enabled me to walk a square block the next morning, only limping a little. By that afternoon, I was able to walk two blocks without limping. A couple of days later, I was walking six blocks without limping; Mark took off the bandage. The next day we walked two miles, and I did not limp at all. However, on November 13, Conan and I played again. He jumped on my back, and I squealed and held up my left front foot for a while. I didn't limp, but Mark wrapped it with two pieces of cloth just to be sure. He ordered a brace from Chewy for me. He left the cloth strips on my leg until the Velcro-brace arrived, and he put it on me. He had to figure out how to wrap it around my foot and make it tight enough not to slip off but not so tight that it hurt. It was stiffer than the cloth strips, and it kept the joint on my foot from bending. I wore it all day long, every day, until Mark took it off at night. I was still wearing it, when I lost it one day. However, a few days later a neighbor spotted it, picked it up, and gave it to Mark.

While all this was going on with my foot, we also had a representative from the internet company fixing Mark's connection. The representative had decided to put in a new cable from the pole to Mark's house and had parked his truck, at which I barked, in Mark's driveway. Mark went out to tell the representative something, and, coming back, hit his head on the ladder cradle which the representative had lowered on the side of the truck. Mark split open his scalp, came into the house to get a towel to put on his head to soak up the blood, went next door to get a neighbor to take him to urgent care, and went across the street to get another neighbor to sit with me and watch his house while the representative went in and out. When he got back, I was watching the representative install a new modem in the house, the neighbor across the street was watching me, and Mark had six staples in his head! I was so happy to see Mark I couldn't be still. Mark held me for a long time, talked to me softly, petted me, and rubbed by belly until I calmed. Mark whispered to me, "It makes me feel very good to be so loved by you."

One day in late November Mark was in the garage repairing the outdoor Christmas decorations in preparation for putting them on the house. I got to be with him and lie in the sun outside the garage door. When it began to sprinkle rain, I came inside and lay on a rug. When it stopped raining, I went back outside. Diarrhea came back with a trip to the backyard and on our morning walk. When we got back, Mark gave me anti-diarrhea medicine with breakfast, lunch, and dinner, and it worked. I was able to sleep through the night, and the diarrhea was gone the next morning. I became very playful, especially when Jared delivered the mail and played with me. I ran around the front yard and back to him, feeling well. However, a few days later, while making a stop at Barbara's house, I threw up my lunch in her front yard. I not only baffled Mark, but I also baffled myself! Mark concluded that I must have eaten something somewhere which upset my stomach. When we got home, he gave me two Pepto Bismol tablets. I was fine after that, eating the rest of my meals, sleeping well, and excited to be alive and have someone who took care of me.

By mid-December 2020, I was very tired. I remember one day on our morning walk stopping and fooling around a lot. Repeatedly, Mark had to say: "Shelby, let's go. Come on!" On our afternoon walk that day, I just stopped and lay on the grass. When I did get up to continue the walk—after a lot of Markan coaching—I moved slowly. After we got home, I ate a dental bone and went to bed and slept for a few hours. After supper and going outside, I went to bed around 6 p.m. Mark said that he thought it was the unusual December heat and humidity that had blown in. Humidity took a toll on me.

On Christmas Eve night, I got up Mark three times to take me outside. I had diarrhea again. Mark told me, "It is caused by the crackers Barbara gave you when we stopped there this afternoon, by the turkey I gave you with dinner, by the rawhide chip you ate, or by something you ate at my friends' house when we stopped there." After the second and third trip outside, Mark gave me a dose of my anti-diarrhea medicine, then a dose with each meal. I didn't want to take it, so he wrapped the tablets in soft food, put them in a little bowl, and brought them to me. Ultimately, I took them. Mark said, "No more of anything that is not on your diet."

By early January 2021, I had had a two-week run with no diarrhea, but I had had no more turkey or rawhide chips either! I was very healthy, walking two miles, one in the morning and one in the afternoon. I was running and playing, especially with Jared. All this was the result of Mark strictly regulating my diet, and it was the result of two walks a day and going to bed every night between 5:30 and 6 p.m.

Also in mid-January, I discovered another activity that I liked to do: sit in the sauna. After Mark opened the sauna in my backyard, I liked getting in and sitting on the bottom shelf for ten to fifteen minutes; the bottom shelf was cool. I had seen Mark go into the sauna on many occasions, and I had been permitted to lie in the anti-room from time to time. Finally, one day, while observing me wanting to look inside the sauna, Mark invited me to come in. Mark, sitting on the top shelf, always tested me to see if I was getting warm. When that occurred, he opened the door and told me to go into the anti-room. Before he got out, he would let me in, while he cooled. Mark said, "Shelby is a sauna dog!"

I also liked walking to a garden north of where we lived. The paths through it are made of mulch, which felt good on my feet! Mark picked out a mile walk for us after lunch which took us through the flower garden. Not only did meandering through the garden make me happy, but taking different routes with all their different smells gladdened me also. The result of my contentment was manifest in listening and doing what Mark told me to do. If he told me to stop so he could give me a drink of water, I stopped. If he told me to stay in a room at Barbara's house, for instance, I stayed in the room. If he told me to wait when he stopped to pick up my poop, I stopped and waited. In the house, when he called me to come to him, I came, no matter what I may have been doing.

I also had a canny sense of time, which fascinated Mark. I often awakened him at 5:30 a.m., when he wanted to get out of bed. In the afternoon I could find him around 3 p.m. to get my dental bone. After eating the bone, my favorite of all the food I got, I often took a nap; if I didn't fall asleep. I lay on my bed and rested for a while. Around 4:30 p.m. I would find him because it was time for my dinner. The only time I missed anything was when I was sleeping. One day, Mark told me: "You have become quite a rascal companion; that is why I often call you 'Rascal Shelbydog.' I consider myself blessed to have you as my companion."

That doesn't mean that we didn't have our rough spots in the road we travelled together. Most nights both of us slept soundly in our respective beds next to each other. Most nights, I awakened Mark at least once during the night to reach over and pull my blanket over me. I wiggled a lot during the night, and my blanket made its way under me instead of over me. One night in late January 2021, I awakened Mark four to six times during one night either to be covered with my blanket or to be petted. He got so aggravated that he yelled at me, saying: "Stop pawing my bed! Go to bed! Shelby, go to sleep!" I didn't awaken him anymore that night. The next night, after getting up to go get a drink of water, I came back to bed and paused and thought about what he had said. I didn't paw his bed. I went back to my bed and lay down and went to sleep uncovered.

My first trip with Mark occurred in early February 2021. He took me to his hometown; he was doing research for a book, and I was along for the ride. I spent three and a half hours in the back seat watching cars, scenery, and buildings pass by. Sometimes I slept, and sometimes I did not. I had never taken a trip this long before. We spent two weeks in a guest house, which I explored over and over again. Mark brought my old bed along and placed it by his bed. My food and water bowls were in the small kitchen. Several people came by every day for interviews. Of course, while they and Mark spoke, I solicited belly rubs from them! In the morning, we walked on gravel and grass, because we were in the country. In the afternoons, we walked on a trail in the woods. I really liked the trail with all the leaves on it and all the scents I had never smelled before. While we were there, it snowed one night. While I had seen and walked in snow before, it was a different feeling on paws walking on snow-covered leaves. We usually ate lunch in the guest house. However, on most evenings, we walked down the road to a big house, where Mark joined others for dinner; he always brought my bowl with my food in it for me. After dinner, Mark washed the dishes, while others dried them and I lay in the middle of the floor to be sure to see everything that was going on! Then, all of us retired to the living room, where a fire was consuming logs in the fireplace. While the others talked, I lay on a rug in front of the fire and often fell asleep. The only thing I didn't like about the big house was the lack of a window with sun. In the guest house, I had several windows under which I could sunbathe!

Nevertheless, I made friends with Sam, the cook; Kathy, the secretary; Natalie, the directress; and Neva, an assistant. Sam, Kathy, and Neva took turns watching me at times and taking me for walks when Mark and Natalie were gone for a few hours. My favorite part of the big house was the steps to the upper floor. I liked to run of the steps, cross through the upstairs hallway, and come down the steps on the other end. There was a lot to explore in the big house. After two weeks, Mark finished his research, and he loaded up the Jeep and we went home.

After getting home, I readjusted to my regular schedule of walking, eating, and sleeping. It felt so good to be able to sleep in my soft bed again. I liked curling into a ball and burying my nose in the bedding. With the blanket Mark put on me, I was comfortable and cozy and secure. After returning from our two-week trip, Mark got me into a good rhythm: a mile walk in the morning, breakfast, sun time, lunch, a mile walk in the afternoon, dental bone at 3 p.m., dinner, backyard around 5:30 p.m., bedtime between 5:30 and 7 p.m. I was thriving on that schedule.

On April 7, 2021, Mark and I celebrated my ninth birthday. I was happy. I was slowing down a little, as I was now an older dog! Some days I was grumpier than others. Nevertheless, I was taking my daily medicine, which Mark wrapped in soft food and put in a small bowl. I learned that if I didn't lap it into my mouth, breakfast was not coming immediately. Mark gave me lots of freedom as to what I did and where I did it in the house. Usually, I took my medicine on the rug between the dining room and living room, on the front porch in the sunshine, or in the kitchen; I got to decide where. Then, I'd get my bowl of breakfast food in the same spot where I had taken my medicine. Mark would give me a bone, which I took to the front porch, unless I was already there. Then, I would sit in front of the glass door and he would kneel behind me. Together we would watch cars pass on the street. He would talk to me, while he petted my head, scratched my back, massaged my front legs, kissed me, and hugged me. Before getting up and going to his office to work, he would leave a second bone for me on the rug by me.

Mark fed me lunch in the dining room or in the kitchen, wherever I wanted it. I got two Milk Bones after lunch, which I took one-by-one to the front porch to eat. In mid-afternoon I would hear Mark call, "Shelbydog, you ready for a bone?" And I would leave my front-porch post and head to the kitchen, where Mark would be standing with a bag of the dental bones. I would stand and wait, sometimes maybe sit, for him to open the bag and hand me a dental bone. Because they were my favorites, I'd jump up to get it from him. Then, I'd run through the house to the front porch to eat it. Before biting into it, I'd lick it so as to taste it fully. Then, with my paws I'd stand it on its end and bite off a piece and chew and chew in delight.

In early April 2021, after my birthday, we took another trip to Mark's hometown. He had more research to do on the book he was writing, and I went along for the ride. As soon as we got there and he opened the car door for me to jump out, I remembered the place. This time, we were not staying in the guesthouse; we were going to live in the big house. Mark had parked the car at the back of the big house, so I ran through the backyard to the backdoor, where my friends Sam, Kathy, and Natalie greeted me and let me in. I was so excited to see them again. They petted me and talked to me while Mark unloaded the car. After he got everything into our room, he showed me where it was and where my bed was. The rest of the house, especially the stairs, I remembered. In fact, I went up the steps to see Kathy, who had gone back to her office on the second floor. She petted me, and I spent some time with her. That trip was only for three days because I got sick.

The night before we left there to head home, the adults ate rotisserie chicken for dinner. I could smell it, and it smelled very good, but Mark forbade me to have any. However, I watched after they finished eating and brought their plates to the kitchen. Mark brought the leftover chicken, and knowing me too well, put it on the top of a cabinet that was too high for me to reach. One of the diners, however, had a piece of chicken left on her plate, and, not spotted by Mark, put in on a low cabinet. I watched as they finished clearing the table and dished dessert onto plates, took them to the dining room, and sat around the table, leaving the dishes to be washed after dessert. I had followed them into the dining room, but decided that this was my opportunity to get the leftover piece of chicken. Mark would think I was going to get a drink of water. All was well and good until I didn't return to the dining room. Mark knew how long it took me to get a drink, but not hearing me lap water, he came to see what I was doing. And he found me in the middle of the floor chewing on that piece of leftover chicken. He took it away from me, saying, "I hope this does not upset your stomach!" I hung my head in shame.

After dessert was finished and dishes washed, dried, and put away, all went into the living room for a while. I was still shameful for having stolen the piece of chicken. Mark was watching me closely to be sure that I wasn't about to throw up in the house. But the evening passed, and nothing happened. I awoke Mark around midnight, and he took me outside to poop; yes, I had diarrhea from eating the chicken. I awoke him again around 3 a.m. I tried to awaken him around 5 a.m., but he was sleeping so soundly that my paw on his bed went unheeded. I didn't know what to do. So, I went upstairs and pooped on the floor in front of the windows, then I came down stairs and had to poop again on the carpet in front of the main door. When my friends Sam and Kathy came to work shorty after Mark arose, they found the messes I had made. Mark wanted to clean up the messes, but they insisted on taking care of them. Meanwhile, Mark gave me a dose of my anti-diarrhea medicine. He told everyone, "The chicken Shelby stole last night has caused this diarrhea; her stomach cannot handle the fat in it." I didn't eat breakfast that morning. Mark left me with my friends for a few hours, while he went to finish his research. He came back around noon, discovered that the medicine was working in me, and packed. Then, we headed home.

By early May 2021, I was feeling my age. I walked a little slower, and I tottered a little both inside and outside. Nevertheless, I liked to trot a little in the morning in the grass along the sidewalk. In the house, my feet slipped more on the tile floors. While I liked the cold, I hated the heat and humidity, which slowed me down considerably. I found myself slipping on one of the tiled back steps. Mark helped me get up and continue on my way. "Take it slow and easy, Shelbydog," he kept saying. "You don't have to run up the steps." I found it harder and harder to jump into the back seat of the Jeep, when Mark took me for a ride. I may look at the seat through the open car door, back away, walk around a little, and come back with a little run and jump to get in. And even with that I often slipped on the edge of the seat and had to scramble with my back legs to get in. The same was true getting out. The distance between the back seat and the floor seemed to get farther and farther away. On several occasions, Mark lowered the back seat so I could get to the cargo area of the Jeep, where he picked me up and set me down in the driveway. Ultimately, Mark solved this problem by letting me jump into the front passenger seat, which was lower to the floor, and pass between the driver's and passenger's seats to my place in the back seat.

After I turned nine years old, I needed more sleep, anywhere from twelve to fourteen hours. If I get enough sleep, I am able to walk a mile in the morning and a mile after lunch or after dinner. If I don't get enough sleep, I refuse to go on a long walk after lunch or dinner. Mark will take me outside, but after a block or two I either turn around to head home or pull him to a side street which leads us back home by way of a short route. When it is cool, I am full of energy, walking, running, and playing. But I don't let everyone walk me I like to choose who will walk me. While I like our next-door neighbor, I won't go but a block or so with her

In late May, Mark, Dan (a friend of Mark's), and Pam (another friend of Mark's) hosted a garage sale in Mark's garage. I was permitted to be with them in the garage. I remembered from a previous such sale how to welcome customers, to get lots of petting, and how to solicit belly rubs. I like Dan and Pam because they talk to me and pet me. All the greetings of customers, coupled with the high humidity, wore me out. When they closed the garage sale, I went into the house and napped.

While it happens infrequently, there are sometimes when Mark has to get me up early in order to walk me, let me pee and poop, and feed me. When those days occur, I am very reluctant to get out of bed early. Mark says: "Shelby, you need to get up. I need to take you for a walk." Of course, I don't move. Mark says: "Shelby, come on. Let's go." I open my eyes and maybe move a little. "Shelby, please get up so we can get a walk in before I have to go." I yawn. "Shelby," Mark says. Finally and reluctantly, I stand up, stretch, stretch, and stretch, and indicate that I am willing to get ready and go for a walk.

In early June, Mark noticed that when he gave me my flea and tick medicine, I slept more for several days, was extremely lethargic, and seemed to stumble when I walked through the house. While we were out walking, I listened to him talk to our neighbors about the flea and tick medicine they didn't give to their dogs. That is correct; they did not give flea and tick medicine to their dogs for a number of reasons: they didn't think there were fleas and ticks in the city; they thought the medicine was too hard on their dog's liver; they had never considered flea and tick medicine for their dogs. After those conversations, Mark decided to cut mine into two pieces and give me half one day and the other half a few days later. That is what he did on the first and fourth days of July, August, and September. And it made all the difference. The medicine didn't cause the side-effects that I had had before. I was still being protected from fleas and ticks, but not with the force of the dose all at one time.

The major story of my life during my ninth year was about slowing down a lot in the heat and humidity that came where I live in mid-June. It got so hot that Mark moved our longest walk to the first thing in the morning after I awoke between 6:30 and 7:30. He'd carry a bottle of water for me, and we would make stops for me to get a drink. With his right hand he held the bottle of water and poured it into his left hand, from which I lapped it into my mouth. We began to skip the post-lunch walk, and try to get in a half mile walk after dinner. Mark filled my pool, which I loved to get in after a walk in the heat. I would lie with the water covering all of me except my head, get up, walk around in the pool, splash a little, and lie in the water again. After I got out, I'd head for the garage, jump on the bench, and Mark would dry me—back, legs, feet, and tail. I liked being rubbed with the towel. When he was finished, he'd say, "You're done," and I'd jump off the bench and head into the house.

By mid-July 2021, Mark and I had put in place a new schedule to avoid as much heat and humidity as possible. We were going to bed around 9 p.m. after a quick trip to the backyard so I could pee. He would turn on the window air conditioner so our bedroom was very cool for sleeping. He'd get up between 5 and 5:30 a.m., and I would follow around 7:30 a.m. He'd get me ready with harness, bandana, leg brace, and water bottle, and we'd walk a mile or more, making stops for me to pee, poop, and get a drink. Once home, Mark would prepare my medicine in a small bowl and my breakfast in a large bowl. I'd take the medicine, eat my breakfast, and chew on two bones, and spend the rest of the morning on the front porch, lying in the sun until I got hot, getting a drink of water, lying on the cool tile floor, then going back to the sunshine. Either Mark would check on me during that time, or I would check on him. We ate lunch around noon, while Mark watched the mid-day news and weather. If it were hot, we'd take a short walk, only a block or two, but if it were cool, we'd walk three or four blocks. After taking pee and poop breaks, we'd come home, and I'd sleep for a while. I'd get my dental bone at 3 p.m., dinner around 5 p.m., and a short walk, if it were hot, after supper, or a longer walk, if it were cooler, after supper.

Mark became aware of how much he read my body language, that is, my dog talk. Unbeknown to many people, I am very expressive. I have a happy face; with my mouth open, showing my white and clean teeth, with my eyes wide open, and with my ears flipped over and at rest, I'm smiling. I have a sad face; I lie my head on the floor and place my front paws flat on the floor on either side of my head, while my ears are flipped over and as far down as I can get them. When I don't understand something, I point up my ears, with a quizzical look on my face I tilt my head from side to side expecting further explanation from whomever is speaking to me. I demonstrate the pleasure I'm feeling from getting a belly rub in one of two ways. Frist, lying on my side, I point up my ears and roll my eyes back. Second, lying on my back with all four legs in the air, I bend my front paws, letting them hang on the end of my legs, arch my back so I can feel intensely the belly rub, and roll my eyes back. I demonstrate that I am listening, but not ready to act on what I am hearing, by moving my ears up and down and, while looking straight ahead, lifting and lowering my eyes and eyelids. Sometimes I get so lost in my focus that Mark has to yell at me several times: "Shelby! Shelby! Shelby!" He is fond of saying, "I don't think your ears are working, sweetie." I also get bored. And when I am bored, I like to lie down and pretend to eat grass, if we are outside. That gets Mark's attention fast, and he pulls the leash, saying: "Shelby, stop. Stop eating grass!"

11

NEW EXPERIENCES

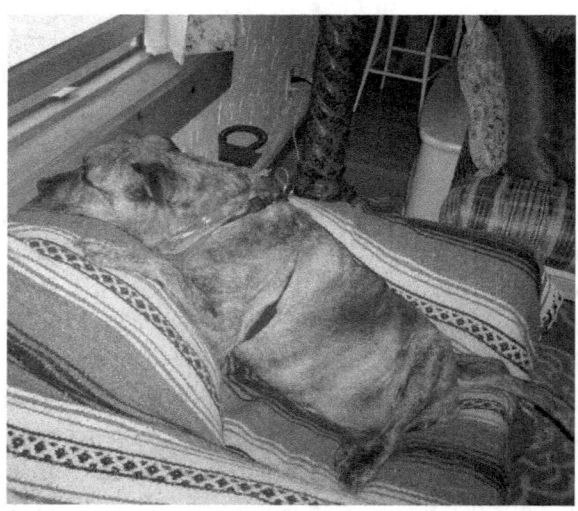

SEPTEMBER, OCTOBER, AND NOVEMBER 2021 featured all kinds of travel for me. Mark had finished his history book, and we began a series of travels to his hometown for book-signing events. In early September, we made our first of three trips to participate in a fall festival. I got to attend the festival, even though I spent most of the day on a leash near Mark in the shade of a tree. Lots of people walked by Mark's booth, buying his books and getting him to sign them. Many times they saw me near him and asked him if they could pet me. He always let them, and I was happy to get the attention. While he seemed to be busy the whole day, he took breaks to talk to me, to feed me, to pour water into my bowl, and to pet me. He got one of his cousins to take me for a walk, but I wouldn't go any farther than I needed to pee and poop before I headed back to Mark. At the end of the day I was very tired and happy to go back to the big house, where we were staying.

After we got home, Mark took me to the backyard after lunch so I could pee one day. He noticed that suddenly I was limping on my right front foot. I know he was ready to panic, when I raised it up and stopped. He bent down to look at it, and a piece of acorn hull fell out from between my toes. He watched me as I put that foot down gently and stepped carefully until I was sure my foot would not hurt anymore. After going in, I enjoyed following Mark from room to room as he swept the floors and ran the vacuum cleaner over the rugs. It was a gray and cloudy day, and I had no sunshine in which to lie. So, I sat on rugs and watched him sweep. I used to be scared of vacuum cleaners and the noise they made, but not anymore. As Mark made his way, he'd have to tell me, "Get off the rug. Move over there," so he could vacuum.

In early October, we headed back to Mark's hometown for another book-signing. Another one of Mark's friends, named Kris, and a friend to me went along for this trip. We arrived at the big house on Friday evening at sundown. I liked being in that big house again; I knew where everything was. I even went upstairs looking for my friend who worked there, but it was Friday evening and she had gone home. On Saturday we ran a lot of errands, picking up chairs, tables, covers, and other things we needed for our booth at the festival the next day. I walked alongside a cart that we used to transport books from the Jeep to the festival grounds where our booth was located. Mark's friend, Kris, was busy posting signs and helping get everything ready. He was also taking care of me so that Mark was free to talk to customers. By mid-morning we were ready. At first, they left me leashless, but I wondered away following my nose. So, after Mark called me back I got leashed near them with a bowl of water. Many people came to visit me, petting me and talking to me. Mark sold and signed many books, and Kris served as cashier. By mid-afternoon it began to rain. So, all the books were boxed and carted to the Jeep, and we headed home. I slept most of the trip home. By the time we got home, I was very, very tired.

By the time I was nine and a half years old, October 7, there were other changes going on with me, most likely age-related. For a while, I didn't want to take my medicine; Mark wrapped it in my favorite soft dog food and put it in a small dish. He would present the dish to me, and I would turn my head to one side or the other. He'd move the dish to under my nose, and I'd turn my head away. He'd move it again, and I'd raise my head to look up. He'd persist until I took the medicine. I stopped eating my breakfast when Mark presented it to me. He would leave it, and I may have eaten it later or not until lunch. All I wanted to eat were the chicken jerky strips.

In mid-October we took a major trip to Colorado. I had never been on a two-day road trip before in the back seat of the Jeep. The longest trip I had ever taken before this one was in a crate from one shelter to another shelter. I didn't like the fact that I didn't have all the back seat to myself; Mark had to put some of our things in a third of it. On the way to Colorado, we stopped to each lunch in a parking lot, and then we continued to Garden City, Kansas. For eight hours I watched cars, took in views, slept, and stretched in the back seat. The hotel room Mark had booked on Expedia did not take pets, although it said it did on the internet. Nevertheless, we found a motel that did take pets, and it didn't take me long to figure out that room. Even I figured out quickly that the place was a dump, but it was a room. Mark discovered that the sink was clogged, so, after seeing the attendant, she gave him a key to another room, where he could use the sink. After we got settled, we went for a walk, making a stop at the Chamber of Commerce, where Mark got a map of Garden City and I got all kinds of petting from the two women in the office. Both of us slept well that night.

The next day, we were on the road at daybreak because we still had a long way to go. When we crossed over Monarch Pass, it was twenty degrees and snowing. I sat in the back seat and watched the snow fall. Before and after Gunnison we ran into light snow again. Then, crossing over the Black Mesa on Highway 92 behind a logging truck, it was like being in a blizzard with snow blowing in all directions and sticking to the ground. After a very slow drive, we got to Bill and Kathy's home. Bill and Kathy are Mark's friends, and they quickly became my friends, too. Mark unloaded the car and got us settled in their guest room, then all of us went for a long walk before drinks for them, treats for me, dinner for all of us, and bed for all of us. I liked sitting in front of their living room glass door that looked to the east, where I could see mountains, lots of wildlife, and the sunrise every morning for the week we were there.

Bill took all of us on a ride to see the colors of the leaves on the trees before they fell off the trees. We made stops at a garage sale, where I got to sniff all kinds of new smells. I got to sit in the back seat with Mark and watch the country go by. He was concerned about how the altitude might affect me, but I adjusted to it well. Because of the cool days at 7,000 feet where Bill and Kathy live, I loved sitting and lying on their deck on the back of their home. There was sunshine there, mountains to see, wildlife to watch, and Bill to follow when he worked in their large backyard. I remember that one day all of us went for a two-mile walk. I had not been on a two-mile walk since the previous winter, when it was cold and there was little humidity. Fall colors, mostly shades of yellow, were in full swing with temperatures in the twenties at night and fifties during the day. I liked that place. I knew where all the doors were located, especially those to the outside deck. I even figured out how to open our bedroom door so I could go see about Bill and Kathy in the morning. They talked to me frequently and petted me often. I heard a lot of new sounds, but the one that kept me awake at night was the whistle of the coal train as it went in to get loaded with coal and out of the area to transport the coal. Another new sound for me was coyote barking.

After a week at Bill and Kathy's home, Mark loaded the car with all our things, and we took a four-hour trip to an apartment over a three-car garage outside Fairplay, Colorado. Mark had booked it for us for the week; he wanted a nice, out-of-the-way place to engage in some editing of his latest book that needed to be polished. After we arrived, he unpacked the Jeep and got us settled. Then, he took me on a walk on a graveled road with woods on both sides. I realized quickly that we were in the country. Mark told me, "Shelby, we are at 9,300 feet here." The only affect the altitude had on me is it quelled my appetite for a few days. One of my favorite friends, Matthew, was in the area, and he came and visited us the next day. All of us walked over a mile on a gravel road.

Two days later, we met Matthew and the rest of his family in Fairplay for an outdoor lunch. Because I was with Mark and Matthew's two small dogs were with him, we needed to eat outside. While all were eating their food, Mark presented mine to me, and I ate all of it, a few small bones, a dental bone, and two chicken jerky strips. Mark applauded and said: "Hurray! Hurray!" After all of us—Matthew's wife and four children—finished eating, we went for a two-mile hike on Beaver Meadow Trail. I loved being outside in the cool, low-humidity air. I jumped over rocks and hurried along the trail. I ignored the small dogs and kept climbing along the trail. We'd stop often, and Mark would give me some water. We got back to the apartment around 2 p.m. I crawled into the over-stuffed chair in which the apartment owner had given me permission to sit to see out the double window, and I fell asleep. When I awoke, Mark said: "You look so cute sitting in that chair, Shelbydog, and looking out the window with your head on the back of the chair. You are becoming a mountain dog."

The next day after lunch, Mark drove the Jeep three miles up the road to a trail head into the Buffalo Mountains. Mark put me on my leash, and he, with walking stick in hand, and I began to walk the trail for about a half mile, when the ice that had frozen to the rocks became too treacherous for both him and me. Both of us were scared of slipping and falling, and he had no cell phone coverage there. Reluctantly, because I was having so much fun in the high country, we turned around in the trees and began our decent slowly over the slick surfaces. Mark kept saying: "Shelby, stop pulling. Slow down." I had four-paw drive, but all he had were two feet with a hiking stick! When we got back to the Jeep, he gave me some water, and then we walked up the road for a good distance before turning around and heading back to the Jeep. When we got back to our apartment, I climbed into the over-stuffed chair and fell asleep. The mountains energized me, but also wore me out. When I awoke, I was hungry, and Mark fed me lots of food.

After all that adventure, another of Mark's friends, John, came to visit. I had never met him before, but I quickly determined that I could get his attention for pettings and soliciting belly rubs. And he did not fail to provide me with such. John and Mark ate lunch, while I ate my lunch. Then, all of us went for a long walk. Where we were staying, autumn had already come and gone, so there was little to no color to see. After the walk, John and Mark talked for a while. Then, John left. That night, I was so excited about the day that I barely slept. I got up after we went to bed and went to the over-stuffed chair and watched outside for a long time. I went back to bed, but couldn't fall asleep, so I went back to the chair. Needless to say, I was tired the next morning.

The day after John's visit was packing day for Mark and resting day for me. I watched as he gathered our things that we wouldn't need for our last night there and put them by the door. Once he had that done, he began carrying everything down the steps and putting all into the Jeep. I followed him down the steps, then up the steps, then down the steps, until I got tired and stopped. There were many snow showers that day, but no accumulation. After getting everything packed, both of us napped.

The next morning, after taking me for a quick walk, we left the apartment and began our trip home. We only stopped for gas and at a rest stop so I could pee. Mark decided that Pratt, Kansas, was far enough. He had driven nine and a half hours over eastern Colorado and western Kansas.

We stopped at the Evergreen Motel west of Pratt. Mark got us a room, and got us settled in it, while it sprinkled rain. Once the rain stopped, Mark walked me over the grounds surrounding the motel and then fed me. We were off the next morning at 7 a.m. after I got a walk. Not too far east of Wichita, it began to rain, and it rained all the way home. Through eastern Kansas, it sounded like a vacuum when Mark passed a truck going the opposite direction on the two-lane roads. The wind would pull the car off the road. The worst part was on Interstate 44; the eighteen wheelers sprayed water like hydras so that I couldn't see through the back windows. Mark slowed down, even though other drivers continued to travel seventy- to eighty-miles an hour. We pulled into our driveway around 1 p.m. I was very hungry, so Mark fed me. Then, while I took my usual position on the front porch, he unloaded the Jeep and put away everything. After dinner, he took me for a walk. Then I went to bed. I was very happy to be home and in my big bed.

After that two-week trip, it took me a couple of days to get back to eating my three meals a day. Gradually, Mark got us back on a schedule of a mile walk after I awoke followed by medicine and breakfast, another mile walk after lunch, a nap, dinner, a quick trip to the backyard to pee, and bed. The cool weather gave me energy to run and play. However, we were not yet finished with travel.

Mark's third trip to his hometown occurred in mid-November. Mark's friend and my friend, Mike, went to a third book signing at a bazaar. We arrived at the big house, where we were to stay. My friends Sam, Kathy, and Natalie greeted me, petted me, gave me a big bowl of water, and made me feel welcome once again. After lunch, Mark and Mike unloaded the Jeep and got us settled. Then Natalie, Mike, Mark and I went for a walk on the trail through the woods. I remembered the ground the trail covered, and I was pleased to be in the lead of the hiking party except when I got distracted by a smell I had to investigate. On Saturday, another friend, Neva, took care of me while Mark and Mike went to the bazaar to sell and sign books. After they got back that afternoon, they took another walk on the trail through the woods. We joined a large group of people on Sunday afternoon for lunch with members of the Old Mines Area Historical Society. I also got to go for a walk on the trails through the Village, a small, uninhabited town of old buildings moved to the historical society's property.

I was really getting into traveling with Mark. After we got home from this trip on Monday, he told me: "There seemed to be less disruption to your schedule, Shelbydog. You followed your usual schedule of eating and sleeping. You ate most of your food and even went to bed by yourself one night. I know you are tired because of all the interaction with many people. You are an introvert, and people wear you out. You look happy to be home and back to our home routines."

By the end of November 2021, Mark was praising me for my cooperation. I felt good. I was free. I had a home. I was trotting on our morning walks. I was always ready to go for a ride with Mark on errands. I was even getting less resistant to getting a bath. Mark understood that when I pawed him, I was showing him how happy I was. I enjoyed our after-lunch walks, no matter how long or short they may be. After we got home, I pawed Mark more, and he responded by playing with me, petting me, and giving me belly rubs. While he cleaned the house, I followed him from room to room. Several times he had to make me get out of the way so he could sweep and vacuum. "You have been a joy to me this day," he told me that evening after we went outside to pee, came back into the house, and I went to bed. "As our bond deepens, I love you more and more," he said to me. I took one of my front paws and put it on his arm, and he knew that I was saying, "I love you, too!"

For Christmas 2021, I received a brand new red and black bandana from Bill and Kathy in Colorado. After Mark gave me a bath on Christmas Eve, he put the new bandana on me. I not only looked good with it on, but I smelled good, too! I was on my best behavior Christmas Eve evening with Barbara, Chris, and Cheryl present for drinks and snacks with Mark. While they ate, drank, and talked to each other, I moved from person to person to receive acknowledgement and petting. Then, I lay down on the rug in the center of them! I had my new bandana on when Mark went to help a neighbor with her cat; he couldn't take me along because I would have chased the cat and at the minimum made the cat very nervous. I always welcomed him back by bringing him my favorite toy—duckie—and running through the house to him.

In early January 2022, Mark took me to Joplin to visit his friend, Art. I had met Art when he visited Mark. In fact, I had nipped Art when he walked up the steps from the basement guestroom without announcing his presence. He surprised me, and I responded accordingly. The nip on his thigh upset him, but he processed it. I had never been to his house before, so I enjoyed exploring every room. I stayed up late with Mark and Art, and Mark took me for walks in Art's neighborhood in Joplin. I had lots of new scents to smell and places to see. While in Joplin, Mark took me to visit Keith and Robin, more of Mark's friends, and they loved me. I got lots of petting and belly rubs. Plus, their large home gave me much to explore. Robin brought me a bowl of water, from which I quenched my thirst.

On a rainy, overcast morning we returned home from Joplin. It wasn't long before I went to my big bed and went to sleep; I slept until mid-afternoon, not even awakening for lunch! It had stopped raining, so Mark took me for a walk. After I ate my dinner, I went back to my bed and slept through the night. Needless to say, I was tired. On those very cold early January days, I joined Mark in the sauna. I loved going out to the sauna in the backyard. It was warm, and I had Mark all to myself!

Often, I join Mark in his home chapel, where he prays. I listen to him read Bible passages. I get a cross traced on my head sometimes. I lie on the rug near the altar and pray. One day Mark said to me: "How like God you are! You want my attention, like God does. You want to play, like God does. You roll on your back in front of the altar, like God does. You want to be loved, like God does. You are free, like God is. You are dependent upon me, like God is. Indeed, Shelbydog, you are a manifestation of the Divine, God present in my house working wonderful deeds." Then, I heard him say a prayer of thanks for all the grace God pours on him and me through the intersession of the Blessed Virgin Mary.

Rain began to fall in early February. The rain turned to freezing rain and ice. Then, it snowed! When Mark went outside to clear the driveway I went with him. As he shoveled areas of the driveway, I followed him, walking only where he had shoveled because I didn't like how deep the snow was. I had to lift my feet and legs too high to avoid getting stuck! When we went for walks, I looked for the sidewalks that had been cleared and headed to them. After it began to warm again, I was getting hot one day in the sun, even though the temperature was only fifty degrees. So, I stopped where there was snow and rolled around in it from side to side and over and over. A few days later, I got some soft snow stuck between my toes on my back right foot. I limped a couple of steps, and Mark lifted my paw and removed the snow from between my toes. And we were back to our mile walk. Another morning after more snow, I walked a half a block, peed, pooped, and turned around to go home. It was very cold and snowing and sleeting, and the only place I wanted to be was in the house.

I like surprising Mark. One evening while he was watching the news, as he usually does, I headed off to bed, as I usually do in the winter months.

He always calls to me: "Shelbydog! Shelbydog! Come here." But I just ignore him and continue my way through the house to our bedroom. He comes in in a few minutes, talks to me, prays with me, kisses me, and spreads my blanket over me. However, one night I changed my mind. When he called, I went over to him and sat next to his chair. He got up and sat on the floor by me. He rubbed my back, scratched my ears, petted my belly, and rolled me around. He made me so happy that I had stopped, but I also made him happy with my companionship. When he was finished loving me, I got up, shook myself, and walked to my bed.

I wasn't so loving a few days later, when Mark awakened me early in the morning. It was sprinkling rain, so he put my coat on me in order to take me outside to pee and poop before he had to leave to keep an appointment. I walked a half block and peed. Then, I planted my four feet, stopping Mark, turned around, and headed back to our house. I took the medicine Mark gave me, but I was not hungry for breakfast. So, I went back to bed. Mark left to keep his appointment. When he got back, it had stopped raining. So, he took me for a mile walk in the cold wind. When I wanted to stop or pause, I developed the practice of planting all four feet, bringing Mark to a stop. He calls it stubbornness; I call it a restful pause! There are days when there are places along the sidewalks that I want to visit before heading home.

The experiences of being halted got Mark to reflect on freedom. He told me: "No one can possess Shelbydog; all I can do is love you. You are free! Some days you are in a very playful mood, finding me, dancing before me, and pawing my legs and feet with your legs and feet. You smile at me, wanting me to follow you to the front porch. You have that mischievous look in your eyes. That is why I refer to you as a rascal. I love it when you find me, sit by my chair, look intently at me, and lie your head on my knee or put your paw on my knee. If I'm asleep in the chair, you put your paw on the footrest repeatedly until you awaken me. I know you want to spend time with me. That is why I sit on the floor with you, petting you, rubbing your belly, and scratching your back and ears. I love lying beside and behind you."

By mid-February 2022, Mark had discovered that he didn't have to say, "Shelbydog, do you want to go for a ride?" All he had to do was pick up the key ring. I could tell by the jingling of the keys that he was getting ready to go somewhere in the car. So, when I heard the keys rattling, I would come running and ready to get into the Jeep.

On the last day of February 2022, Mark was working in his office, and I overheard him reading aloud some words about me. I pointed my ears and stood still on the other side of the door. Here is what I heard: "I see a sixty-pound dog"—that is I—clothed in brindle fur with highlights (streaks) of red that glisten in the sunshine. Three paws are darker than the fourth! Her front toe nails are longer than the back paws due to scratching, marking spots along sidewalks. Often, I see a brindle tail with red streaks wagging left to right with delight when I talk to her. I see brown eyes, clear and bright, a red tongue with black birth marks on it in several places. I see a short, black, wet nose, underneath a full set of clean teeth. I see a light brown to beige belly, which is arched in the air to solicit scratches. I see a dog who gets hot easily when in the sun; she is like a solar panel! I see a dog, who, when she is hot, stops and lies down in a shady spot. I see a dog, who, when hot delays the walk, spends lots of time sniffing bushes, trees, and wild garlic; stopping to roll in leaves, grass, or snow; running when cold; playing by hunkering down and springing into a fast run. I see a dog who runs into the house from the garage through the porch, into the kitchen, through the dining room and living room, and to the front porch to stretch out on the rug before the door in the sun."

I listened as he continued reading: "I see a dog who gets too hot in the sun and moves to another rug out of the sun. I see a dog who has a happy face, a sad face, an excited face, an all-is-OK face, and a I'm-going-for-a-ride face. I see a sleeping dog on her belly, on her side, stretched from one end of her bed to the other. I see a dog who can make herself big or curl up and make herself small, who likes to be covered with her blanket at night or during a nap in the daytime. I see a dog who looks for her toys—duckie, dearie, square—to bring to whomever comes to the front door but wants it returned as soon as he or she takes it in hand. I see a dog dreaming of running as her legs and feet move in harmony, while she is sleeping on her side. I hear little groans or faint barks as she chases rabbits and cats in her dreams. I see a dog who comes to find me when she hears loud thunder or just to see what I am doing wherever I am doing it. I see a dog who likes to wear a bandana every day; it is my responsibility to choose one from her wardrobe. I see a dog who stretches repeatedly before taking a walk, and I hear a dog who grunts when stretching and growls gutturally when someone walks by outside, who barks when other dogs bark, even though she cannot see at what they are barking, or who barks when any delivery truck rolls along the street or someone comes to the front door. I hear a dog squeal with delight when she gets something she really wants, like a ride, a walk, a dental bone, a belly rub, etc." Mark said all that about me, Shelbydog, and I was amazed at how well he knew me.

One morning in early March 2022, Mark took me for a morning walk in the snow. As we made our way over the mile walk, the snow gathered on my coat and nose and eyelashes. I trotted in the soft flakes that covered my four feet. It was so quiet in the falling snow. That same day, after Mark shoveled the path to the sauna, he spent an hour in it in the afternoon, and I got to spend about ten minutes at the beginning and the end. It was like the end to a perfect day. After we came back into the house, I heard Mark reading aloud again. He said: "I smell a dog"—that's me again—"fresh from her bath with the scent of her shampoo coming from her fur. I smell a dog who needs a bath, like old olive oil, rancid, or spoiled canned dog food. I smell the scent of shampoo reactivated by rain sprinkles on a dog's head. I smell the fresh scent of rain on her. I smell the musty scent of a dog who eats lamb and rice kibbles. I smell the chicken and turkey and venison of her canned food. I smell her scent on the rugs upon which she lies, upon her bed, and upon her blanket."

He continued: "I feel a wet dog, who wiggles and moves a lot after getting wetted with the shower nozzle in preparation for a bath. I feel the slick shampoo as I rub it into her fur until she is soaped over her head, back, butt, tail, belly, legs, and feet. I feel her slick coat as I run fresh water all over her to rinse the soap out of her fur, not stopping until the water runs clear into the drain. I feel her lips on my fingers when she takes a bone from my hand or she brings her face close to mine and smells me and exhales a puff of air on my face at the same time. I feel her damp feet and the damp fur between her toes after we have walked in the rain or snow and I take a towel to dry them after we go inside. I feel her soft fur after she thoroughly dries after a bath. I feel her tug and pull and squirm when getting a bath or walking on the end of the leash."

On another day, Mark became aware again of my sense of my size. He noticed as I examined spaces and determined which I could get into and which I could not. I didn't have to try to get into a space; I knew whether or not I would fit. I knew I could walk under the dining room table among the chairs without getting stuck. I knew I could not get into the space between the lounge chairs in the living room. Even outside, I knew which bushes I can squeeze behind or through and not get stuck.

Mark told me: "Shelby, I cannot taste you! However, I hope that what you taste is what I taste, when I share a small morsel of food from my plate to your bowl at dinner time." While he taught me not to beg by raising his first finger to indicate one—meaning that he was giving me the last bone for a given meal—at dinner time he always provided two or three more bites of very small bones and a morsel or two from his plate in my bowl after I ate my last bone. This action made me feel special. Then, he would say to me, "Go get a drink," and I would trot off to my water bowl in the kitchen or the one on the front porch. Yes, I had two bowls always full of water!

12

TENTH BIRTHDAY

A MONTH BEFORE I was going to turn ten years old, in other words on March 7, 2022, Mark was working in the garage and I was lying on the driveway. The substitute mail carrier walked up the driveway, and I sprang to my feet barking with hackles raised. That made the mail carrier, whom I knew, stop. Mark said: "She won't hurt you. Just let her smell you." That calmed him, as I approached to smell him. He petted me, and all was well as Mark came forward to get the mail. I heard Mark tell him: "I don't know how to make her not raise her hackles. I think it has something to do with invading her space, but I'm not sure." The fact is that those erectile hairs along my back arise when I am alarmed. It is pure instinct, and nothing more.

I loved the early days of March because it was so cool outside. If Mark and I got our two one-mile walks in earlier in the day, Mark took me to the back yard. "Let's go outside and go pee-pee," he would say, and I would lead him to my favorite spot to do so. After I peed, I walked around the perimeter of the yard smelling everything. If it were cool, I might begin to run and play jumping over the railroad-ties that outlined the flower beds. Then, I would head for the garage with a happy smile on my face. Mark would follow and let me into the house. I'd run up the back steps into the kitchen, through the dining room, through the living room, and to my room on the front porch. There, I would find my rug and lie on it in front of the door.

The first thunderstorms of spring always frightened me. Once it began to rain, thunder and lightning followed. I would leave my place in front of the door and move to the living room rug. I remember Mark taking my living room pillow and putting it by his chair while he watched TV. "Come and lie over here," he said. And that is what I did. I stretched out on the pillow, and he covered me with my living room afghan, and I fell asleep for almost two hours. Even though the thunder and lightning continued outside, I felt safe inside by Mark.

One thing that I never liked was changing time in early March. It messed with my circadian clock. More daylight caused me to stay up later, and then I stayed in bed later the next morning until my rhythms got in sync again. It took two to three weeks for me to adjust. With the longer daylight at the end of the day, instead of going to my bed, I often fell asleep on the front porch. When Mark was ready to go to bed, he would call, "Shelby, it's time to go to bed," and I would arise, walk to our bedroom, and lie on my bed for the rest of the night.

I loved going with Mark on errands. I remember one day where we drove around town for several hours. Because it was cool outside, I stayed in the back seat of the Jeep. Sometimes I just watched cars and people come and go from parking lots; at other times I lay on the back seat and napped. When I heard the automatic car door locks disengage, I knew Mark was getting into the Jeep, and I would sit and welcome him back.

By mid-March 2022, I was having some inflammation in my joints, but Mark did not know about it. He noticed that I was walking a lot slower than usual, even though it was not hot. I dawdled a lot. I looked for shade. I rolled in the grass. I stopped to rest. I stopped to get a drink of water from the bottle Mark always carried. After we got back from walks and I cooled, Mark would sit with me, and I would let him see into my soul, breathe my spirit, touch me deeply. He thought my slowness was due to my stubbornness. "I want to hear your spirit," he said. "I see you becoming more secure in being yourself, who you truly are, but your stubbornness is getting in the way." It wasn't stubbornness at all; I was in pain.

The pain seemed to intensify when it rained. Spring of 2022 was very wet and cloudy. One day in mid-March we couldn't get outside until almost 2 p.m. Mark put my coat on me, and we headed out into a light, misty fog. We walked about two blocks, and because my joints were hurting, I turned around and started back home. Mark didn't know that I was in pain. So, he pulled the leash to get me going again. We repeated that scenario several times, until I just decided to walk the mile. "Stop being so stubborn," Mark kept saying. I was not being stubborn; I was in pain.

In late March, Mark decided to renew my bed. About two years before, he had taken out the stuffing with which it came when it was new, and replaced it with several old pillows. However, those had flattened and moved over the year, so he purchased memory foam and replace the pillows with two layers of that wonderful bedding. But, because I loved to scratch my bed before I got into it—an instinct from my wolf ancestors when preparing a den—I had broken the top layer of foam into small pieces, which were coming out of the bed and spreading all over the floor of our bedroom. Mark took apart my bed, kept the one intact piece of foam, threw way the bits and pieces, and washed the bed. After it dried, he sewed denim on both sides of the cover. Then, he placed an old blanket on top of the single layer of memory foam, and I had a new bed. The denim made it stiff and not as soft as it was before. He followed me into the bedroom that night and said, "I don't want to hear you scratching your bed." It took me a few days to get used to the stiffness; now I appreciate what Mark did for me.

By the end of March, the inflammation of my joints was getting worse, but Mark wasn't able to hear what I was telling him. Our morning walks didn't bother me too much, but the afternoon walks really hurt me. We would walk a few blocks, and I would turn around and want to go home. Mark would give me a drink of water, tug me to get me going again, and tell me how stubborn he thought I was being. On drier days, the pain was not as bad as on wetter days. Before my birthday in early April, on low humidity days we often walked two miles, one in the morning and one after lunch. I got to roll in the cool green grass and run and play. With a big smile on my face I would find Mark in the house, bring him my toys, and lead him to a rug, where he would play with me for a while. The sunshine made me very happy; I spent hours lying in the sun on the front porch.

On April 7, I marked my tenth birthday, approximately sixty-six or sixty-seven in dog years! "Happy birthday, Shelbydog," Mark said several times during the day. He gave me a new cloth bone for my birthday. I love to take those apart. I spent some time pulling the threads from the side of the bone. Then, I was able to get pieces of stuffing out, while lying on a rug. I pile the stuffing on either side of me, blowing breath out of my mouth to push it away. My joy is finding the plastic squeaker inside and putting it in one pile of the stuffing. After playing with it for a while, I'd stop and leave it. Mark would come around and pick it up, throwing away the stuffing I had removed and putting what was left of the toy in my toy box. Later, on other days I'd get it and remove more stuffing. Finally, when all that was left was a rag, I'd keep it in my box. Mark tried to throw away previous cloth-bones-that-became-rags, but I always retrieved them from the trash can!

I also got three new bandanas for my birthday. Every day I wear a bandana. After Mark puts my harness on, I stick out my nose so he can put on my bandana. Over the years many different people have given me bandanas of all colors. I have a whole drawer full of them. Mark gave me a yellow one, a multi-colored, tied-dyed one, and a solid red one. Those were added to my red, green, blue, and pink wardrobe.

A few days after my birthday, Mark was cleaning the house room by room. I like being with him, sitting on the rugs, watching him sweep and vacuum. We were in the bedroom. He picked up my bed and moved it in order to clean under it. I put on a sad face. He told me, "I'll put it back as soon as I've finished cleaning." I watched closely, until he put it back where it belonged near his bed. Then, I went to it and stretched out on it, while he continued to clean the room.

That same day we had a new mail carrier, one neither Mark nor I knew. Because I couldn't smell him, I barked and barked until Mark came to see what was going on. After Mark opened the door, I stuck out my head and he petted me lightly. He was in a hurry; it was already 5:30 p.m., and he had a lot of mail yet to deliver. After Mark closed the door and locked it, he turned around to see me sitting behind him with my duckie in my mouth. He said, "You look so sad, sweetie." He petted me and talked to me for a while. I liked giving duckie to our mail carrier, who had to give it back to me quickly. Mark petted me and rubbed my belly for a while to cheer me.

On April 18, 2022, I was sad again after Mark's friend and my friend, Matthew, left. He comes every year for a few days. I like him. I let him walk me. And he spends time petting me and talking to me. I got to ride in the Jeep when we went to get him at the airport a few days before, and I got to go again when Mark took him back to the airport to catch his plane. After we got back, Mark tried taking me for a walk, but I turned around and headed back home. Mark tried getting me to take a nap, but I didn't want to do that either. Yes, I was sad, but my joints were hurting, too. Mark attributed my noncooperation to the humidity, and rightly so to some degree. On a walk a few days later, I snapped at another dog for no reason. I had been stopping and rolling in the grass, stopping and rolling, stopping and rolling, and Mark was getting upset. "Please come on, Shelby," he would say. "I think your age is affecting your behavior." One afternoon, he felt so bad because he had to coach and tug me home, that he came to my bed and said, "I'm sorry, Shelbydog," and he kissed me several times on the head. Again, he did not know that I was in pain.

The next day he told me: "As I have reflected on the past two months, I've come to a deeper understanding of why your first family left you in a shelter when they moved. You are often mean to some dogs, snapping, growling, trying to bite them. You are supremely stubborn, refusing to walk in the direction indicated, suddenly stopping in the middle of the street, refusing to move, suddenly lying and refusing to get up, stopping and planting your four feet when not getting your way. You don't obey; I told you to stop scratching your bed, but you continue to do it. You shredded the rug in the basement after I caught you doing it and told you to stop. You don't listen; when called, you continue to walk away. Your general stubbornness about anything makes you very undesirable. I also want you to know that I understand that you are a very free spirit, and I am still trying to understand you better." Needless to say, I was caught off guard by what Mark said. At that point it was clear to me that he did not yet know that I was in pain.

Very early in May another of Mark's friends, Marcia, came to visit. Mark had awakened me at 6:30 a.m. to go on a walk before it began to rain. After we got home from the walk, he fed me breakfast, after which I lay on the front porch. Once it began to rain, I went back to bed. Once Marcia arrived, I sought her attention the whole time she was with us. I hoped she would figure out what was going on with me and tell Mark. However, that did not happen. To display my repentance for supposedly not cooperating with Mark, I took a nap on my bed that afternoon, while he took a nap on his. We spent more time together that afternoon. Later, while he was reading, I went to his chair and sat by him. I went to bed around 7:30 p.m.

My sun lamp arrived in early May. Mark bought it for me, hoping that it would help my mood on cloudy days. While it does not produce heat, it does shine sun-like rays on me, when I stretch out under it. Two or more cloudy, dreary days in a row make me sad. The sun lamp functions like the sun, pouring rays on my head and back and side. It is a wonderful gift to receive.

Also, another incident set in motion a series of events that got Mark to comprehend the pain I was in from my joints. On Mother's Day, he took me for a walk, even though it was warm. The walk got cut short two blocks from home. After I pooped and he was bent over picking it up in a plastic bag, I began to move forward and slipped somehow. I squealed. He turned around to see me standing on three legs with my left front paw held up. He looked it over, searching between my toes to see if I had something stuck in there, but he could not find anything. He bent my foot a little so he could see better, and I barked and cried. He made me lie on the grass so as to better see my foot, but, upon examination, he could find nothing. He urged me to get up, but I could not put any pressure on that left front foot.

Thank goodness we were just a few steps from the front gate of a house in which lived people we know. Mark led me hobbling through the gate to the front porch. He got one of the people who live there to come to the door. He asked the man to hold and watch me while he walked home the two blocks to get the Jeep and come and get me. That man was very nice to me. He held onto my leash and talked to me and petted me. Meanwhile, Mark went home, got the Jeep keys, and came to get me. I hobbled out of the yard and to the Jeep, was able to jump into the front seat, and Mark took me home.

When we got home, I was able to get out of the Jeep and move up the back steps very slowly into the house. Mark followed me, saying: "That is the same foot you sprained a couple of years ago. I'm going to find the brace that we used then and put it on you." He left for a few minutes to look through my things, and then he returned with the brace and put it on my foot. The brace supports my foot and leg and eliminates some of the pain of putting my weight on it. After taking a nap that afternoon, I was able to navigate the back steps to make a trip to the back yard to pee after supper. Mark left the brace on until I went to bed.

The next day I slept late, but when I did get up, I wasn't limping. Mark got me ready for a very short walk by putting on my harness, bandana, and foot brace. Then, we walked for about a block and a half; I peed and pooped and we returned home. "We're taking it easy today," Mark said. He took me to the back yard after lunch. After supper, we walked a block. He said to me: "Your pain, Sweetie, causes me great distress and concern because we are so close to each other. I pray for your healing. I pray that God will show mercy to you, his servant. I love you very much, and I cannot stand to see you suffer in light of all the suffering you have endured throughout your life."

Over the next few days, my foot continued to get better, and we walked only a few blocks, usually one in the morning and two after supper with the brace on. The humidity was high, and Mark knew that I do not respond well to it. Add to that the summer time temperatures, and both of us were feeling drained by the heat. Finally, it cooled and normal spring temperatures returned. By the end of the week, my foot was well-healed, and I demonstrated it by trotting a little as we extended our walks. With the humidity gone and my foot healed, I played with Mark.

He calls it a dance. With a happy face I quickly and repeatedly place one paw over the over while touching Mark's leg or foot. Then, I turn and begin to run but look back to see if he is following me. If he does, I lead him to a rug and lie on it. He kneels beside me and pets, talks, and rubs my belly. I giggle with delight. If he does not follow me, I go back to him and do my dance again. Later that day, I heard Mark describe my dance. Then, he began to describe my many facial expressions. I listened to what he said.

"Shelbydog, you have a happy face; your mouth is open, your teeth are showing, your eyes are wide open, your ears are flipped over at rest, and you are smiling. You show your sad face, when you place your head flat on the floor with your front paws flat on the floor on either side of your head with your ears flipped over at rest. When you don't understand something I'm telling you, your ears point up with a quizzical look on your face and your head tilting from side to side. You also have a pleasure face; during belly rubs, you put your head on its side, your ears are pointed up, and your eyes roll to the back of your head. You have a posture of listening but not being ready to act; you move your eyes and ears up and down, and you look straight ahead."

A week after I hurt my foot, the next part of Mark's understanding began. It was early Sunday morning, nice and cool. We went out for our morning walk. We walked by two of our friends sitting on their porch in their pajamas and sipping coffee. We had to cross the street to say hello to them. He is a veterinarian, so he asked about the brace on my foot. Mark told him. He said, "There may be some arthritis in that foot." And that got Mark to thinking. We walked a mile that morning, and I began to slow down on the last half mile. Mark attributed it to the humidity at first, but the word *arthritis* continued to come to his mind. Because it rained a lot that day, we didn't get out again until mid-afternoon in the sprinkling rain. That was the first time I ever walked in the rain without my coat. I usually turn around as soon as a feel a raindrop, but it felt so good on my skin after three or four days of hot weather that I continued. After we got home, Mark took a towel and dried me from nose to tail and between all my toes.

Remember, Mark was thinking about the possibility of me having arthritis. However, he was trying to distinguish the effect the humidity had on me and the pain I was having that he didn't know about. He watched me slow down for the last few blocks on early morning walks. He began to notice that I was struggling to keep moving. He noticed that I was limping a little. I saw him go online and read about arthritis in dogs and conclude that maybe that is what I had. I had been cutting short our after-lunch walks and our after-dinner walks by heading home after only a block; I slowed down more and more and stopped often to lap water from Mark's hand. Finally, Mark called my vet and scheduled an appointment to find out what was happening to me.

Between the scheduling of the appointment and the appointment day, I was in great pain. I manifested it by awakening Mark at 5 a.m. with my paw on his bed. Then, I went to the rug by the bedroom door and sat facing it. That meant that I wanted to go outside, so Mark got up and took me outside to pee in the sprinkling rain. After the rain stopped, he took me for a short walk. After we got back and I ate breakfast, I went to the front porch for a while, then back to bed. After lunch we walked one square block. He didn't think I was in pain because I was eating my three daily meals and playing with him all the while experiencing pain in my joints. On cool mornings, the pain was not as severe as it was on hot afternoons or evenings. I usually walked a mile on cool mornings with only a few stops for water. On very cool mornings, I even trotted a little. The walking and trotting were good for me; I know that. The day before my appointment with my vet I walked a total of two and a fourth miles; it was only sixty degrees outside.

In late May, Mark took me to see my veterinarian. I always get nervous going into her clinic and more nervous waiting for her in one of the small patient rooms. I walked around the room a lot, even though I was in some pain. Mark tried, and often succeeded, in quieting me by telling me to sit still or lie on the floor near him while he petted me. Finally Heidi came in to see me. She examined my joints and told Mark, "I think she is in some pain because of the inflammation in her joints." She explained to Mark that she was going to devise a plan of treatment for me. The first step in the plan was a two-week regimen on an anti-inflammatory drug called Carprofen; Mark was instructed to give it to me two time a day for two weeks. After a week on the Carprofen, Mark was instructed to contact Heidi and report what he observed about me.

I took my first dose of Carprofen with my dinner the same day I had seen the vet. After I got up the next morning, I noticed that I was feeling much better. The inflammation was decreasing, and my pain was decreasing with it. Two days later, I was walking, trotting, and running throughout our mile morning walk. And four days later, I felt like running most of the two and a half miles we walked that day in three different outings. Then, the humidity returned, and I slowed down. But Mark knew now that it was the humidity that was slowing me and not my joints. I felt like my old self again. "I have my old Shelbydog back," I overheard Mark tell someone we see regularly on our walks.

After he filed his report with my vet, we took a trip to the vet's clinic to get the new drug that Mark opted to give me. It is called Dasuquin Advanced. It is a soft chew one step above the Cosequin I have been taking daily for three years. It is designed to restore my joints. Restoration takes place with Dasuquin while inflammation is kept at bay with Carprofen. I overheard Mark tell my vet, "I can tell how happy Shelbydog is. She has even been sleeping better. I want to do what is right for her."

The night after we saw the vet, Mark followed me to my bed to pray with me and cover me. "I didn't know that you were in pain. I didn't know that you were suffering. I am so sorry. I love you so much." And he hugged me. He attributed my struggle and limping to the humidity, and the humidity is responsible for some of it. However, inflammation in my joints is responsible for some of it, too. Now, I'm back to feeling better, walking, trotting, running, and playing. I'm back to being a free spirit whom Mark loves. I'm back to being a free spirit who loves Mark and all he has done for me.

13

MORE TRAVELS AND ADVENTURES

Mark and I left Springfield and headed to Fertile near the end of June 2022 on a Wednesday. I like getting into the Jeep, especially when I have all the back seat to myself. However, this time we had so much cargo that I got only two-thirds of the back seat because one-third was folded down to accommodate the cargo we were transporting. I got to see my friends: Sam, Kathy, Natalie, Neva, and Ernie. Mark got us settled into our usual room, and I went with him on a walk through the woods. We enjoyed a quiet afternoon in one of my favorite places to visit.

The next day, Thursday, Sam volunteered to take care of me, while Mark went to a luncheon meeting of the Washington County Chamber of Commerce. He gave them a presentation on Philippe Francois Renault, the founder of Old Mines in 1723. Since I didn't go along, I do not know what he said. I do know that he was back before 1 p.m., and then he and Natalie left to go visit his sister, Jane, who was in a hospital. I stayed with Sam, until she went home, and then by myself for a while. Once alone, I began in our room and pushed all the pillows off of the bed. Then, I went to the living room and pawed all the pillows off of the sofa and loveseat there. I went upstairs to one bedroom and pulled all the pillows off of one guest bed. So, by the time Mark got home, I had made my way through the house tossing all the pillows onto the floor in protest at having been left alone! Once Mark got back, he went through the house and gathered all the pillows and replaced them.

On Thursday evening, Mark and Natalie had rotisserie chicken for dinner. I stood in the kitchen smelling it and watching Mark cut it into pieces on a platter. I took note of where it was sitting by the sink, after Mark and Natalie put chicken and vegetables on their plates and went to the dining room to sit down at the table and eat. Neither of them noticed my absence from the dining room. Once they were gone, I studied carefully how high the shelf was by the sink, and I judged that I could jump and place my front paws on it and grab a piece of chicken! What I didn't calculate was the lip on the platter. When my front paws landed on the edge of the counter, they tipped the platter; it flew over, sending chicken pieces and itself onto the floor. The platter shattered into hundreds of pieces, and chicken parts were spread over the kitchen floor. At the sound of the crash, Natalie and Mark ran to the kitchen just as I was making my escape from that room. It took them only a few seconds to conclude what had happened. Mark picked up the chicken pieces, got a broom, and began to sweep up the shards of what had been a platter. Natalie got a mop, whetted it, and cleaned up the chicken juices on the floor. I sneaked into the dining room to avoid any conflict. Once my mess was cleaned, Mark and Natalie went back to the dining room to finish their dinner. Later, Mark removed the skin from the leftover chicken pieces and put them in a plastic container for Sam to use to make chicken salad the next day. I didn't get into much trouble that

Thursday evening, as I was more scared of the crash that the platter made when it hit the kitchen floor.

The next day, Friday, was a rest day. Mark read and worked on a talk, and I trotted from room to room to visit my friends. In the afternoon, Mark wanted to take me on a walk through the woods, but the heat and humidity made me turn around and head back to the cool house. Because I was taking my medicine, the inflammation in my joints was decreasing, and my Dasuquin Advanced was restoring movement, enabling me to trot, run, and walk up and down stairs with ease.

More of the same took place on Saturday. However, on Sunday I was left alone again while Mark and Natalie went to church. I had three hours to roam through the big house and go from room to room pushing and pulling pillows off of beds, sofas, and chairs. Mark got home first, and he went from room to room tidying all the pillows. Again, I didn't get into too much trouble, as Mark knew that I didn't like being left alone. On Monday, Mark packed the Jeep, I climbed in, and we headed home.

The last day of July 2022, Mark took me to Joplin, Missouri, where I stayed a few hours with one of my favorite people, Mike. While Mark was taking a friend of his to lunch/dinner, Mike was taking me on a walk and playing with me. He is one of the few people I will let walk me! I had never been to his house before, so I had a good time smelling around every room and rolling on the rugs. Later in the afternoon, Mark came and got me and took me home.

About a week later, Mark took me with him to a friend's house in Springfield. I was on my best behavior, obeying all Mark's directives and not pestering the other three people there for belly rubs. On the way home, Mark said, "Shelby, you were so good this evening; I am proud of you." After we got home, Mark took me on a short walk in the humid heat so that I could pee and poop before going to bed.

One day in mid-July 2022, Mark found me stretched out on the front porch. He said: "I have suddenly become aware of how happy you make me, Shelbydog. When I see you looking at me with your tail wagging, I am very happy. When I see you all hunkered down and ready to go on a walk, I am very happy. When you come to the dining room ready to eat or to the kitchen to get a bone, I see your happy face, and that makes me happy. Knowing that you have no joint pain and seeing you be your rascal self, rolling on the grass or on the large rug in the living room, fills me with joy.

When someone comes to the front door and you bring your duckie toy to him or her, he or she is usually happy, and that makes me happy."

Indeed, I was so happy in July that on the foreordained day of my bath I met Mark at the top of the steps and went into the bathroom. I was ready for my bath before he was; he needed to get the extra rugs he puts on the floor and my towels, soap, and other things. Once he was ready, I lay in front of the shower, as I usually do, and he, picking up my front paws and putting them in the shower, lifted by back legs and scooted me in. Then, he followed the usual procedure for a Shelbydog bath.

On July 30, 2022, Mark was packing the Jeep for our longest adventure of the summer. For weeks before that date, he had been gathering all kinds of things and putting them in cases and bags in preparation for us to be gone a month to Colorado. I enjoyed watching him take all the items from the sunporch to the garage and load them into the Jeep. I thought that we were leaving that day; I was ready to go! However, we didn't leave until the next day. After Mark took me for a long walk, he finished packing and closing the house. I climbed into the two-thirds of the back seat that I was allotted for this trip, and we left Springfield. On the way to Garden City, Kansas, we stopped at a rest stop, where Mark gave me water and food, which I didn't want. After getting to the motel he had booked in Garden City, Mark fed me and went to get his dinner at a restaurant next to the motel. I stayed alone for about thirty minutes and behaved myself. When Mark returned, he ate his dinner, and he gave me a few bones to top off mine.

That evening, while Mark was reading and I was lying on the floor, he called my name and patted the edge of the bed upon which he was sitting, indicating that I had permission to jump onto the bed and lie down. I did. And I enjoyed being so close to Mark that after he went to bed, I jumped on the other side near the foot and slept there all night. He didn't make me get off the bed and sleep in my bed, which he brought along. That was the very first time I had ever slept by him.

The next day we arrived at our apartment eight miles outside of Fairplay, Colorado, where we were staying for the month of August. After getting there in early afternoon, Mark spent the time hauling our things up the steps to the apartment, located over a three-car garage, and then putting away everything: clothes, food, and my things, such as bed, medicine, and food. After all was done, Mark took me for a walk. I remembered the place from last October, when we spent a week there. In the early evening, it thundered and rained. Of course, the thunder sounds loud because it echoes off of the mountains. I was scared and sat on a rug by the couch, where Mark was sitting. He leaned over frequently and petted my head, saying, "Nothing is going to hurt you."

Because it was still thundering when we went to bed and I was still afraid, Mark motioned for me to jump onto one side of the large bed to sleep. I walked around the bed several times determining the best place to jump onto it, because it was a tall bed. After watching me for a while, Mark took my front paws and placed them on the edge of the bed, then he lifted my back legs and scooted me to the place I would sleep. Then, he covered me with my blanket. Not only did I feel warm and cozy, but I felt secure next to Mark. I awakened him around 5:40 a.m., when I saw daylight streaming into the window.

Over the next few days, we settled in to our month-long residence, went into town to do some shopping and to fill the Jeep with gasoline. Because the sun was shining on the landing—a little porch or stoop—at the top of the stairs at the door, I wanted to go out there and lie in the sun. Mark opened the door and let me go to the porch, saying, "Do not go down the steps." Of course, something got my attention in the grass, and I jumped down the steps. Mark came to the door, looking for me. Not finding me, he stepped onto the porch and caught sight of me at the bottom of the steps getting ready to make my ascent. Again he said, "Don't go down the steps." A while later, he came to check on me again, but I had descended the steps and was trotting down the road, when I heard, "Shelby, get back her NOW!" A couple of days later, he bought a leash in town that he could attach to the railing around the porch and to me to keep me from wandering off of the porch. After a couple of days of being tied on the porch, I got the message: I could lie in the sun, but I could not descend the steps.

On our fourth morning in the apartment, the temperature was 57 degrees outside. A cold rain had fallen the night before. The temperature inside the apartment was 61 degrees. Mark couldn't get the stove to come on to warm us. Nevertheless, he got me ready and took me for a walk after he put on his jacket and cap. While we walked the road, Janet, the proprietor of the apartment, drove by and stopped. Mark told her that we had no heat. She explained that lightning the night before had knocked out the electricity, and the pilot on the stove needed to be restarted. So, she turned around, came in, and got the pilot started. Then, we had heat. I stretched out on the floor in front of the stove until it warmed up a little.

On the evening of August 4, 2022, Mark tucked me into my bed, then he got ready to get into his bed. After he climbed in, I decided that I wanted to sleep next to him again. So, I jumped up to the empty place. He got up grabbed by blanket, and covered me. I liked sleeping next to Mark so much that I jumped to that spot every evening while we stayed in the apartment. He was careful not to roll onto me, and I was careful not to roll onto him.

A couple of days into our month stay, I developed some diarrhea. Mark didn't know what was causing it. I had no new food. The only thing different was the bottled water, which was necessary because tap water contained sulfur. I was also getting a lot more intense sun at this 9,300-feet elevation. It was an occasional diarrhea, and, as usual, when I have diarrhea, I don't eat all my food and don't want to take my medicine. Mark tried giving me my prescription anti-diarrhea medicine, but that didn't seem to work. So, we went to the Dollar General store, where he bought Pepto-Bismol, Immodium AD, and some large bottles of water. He gave me several doses of the Pepto-Bismol, but that didn't stop the loose bowels. So, he gave me several doses of Immodium AD, and that worked. Then, he took my medicine and wrapped it in soft dog food so I would take it. I, of course, would move my head from side to side and up and down to avoid the little bowl with the medicine in it, but sooner or later I'd take it.

I think that Mark figured out that it was this place that caused my anxiety and diarrhea. I was at first insecure here, even though we spent a week here last October. Over the next few days, as we got into a routine, I became more comfortable.

On day six of our month-long stay in Colorado, some of Mark's friends came to visit him and me. There was John, the dad; Amy, the mother; and Ethan and Jacob, the sons. All of us piled into John's truck—Amy, Ethan, and Jacob in the back, and Mark and me sharing the passenger seat with John driving. We traveled only about three miles to the Rich Creek trailhead, where we hiked in the Buffalo Peaks Wilderness area. While Mark had my leash in his hand at the beginning, it wasn't long before I let Ethan and Jacob walk me. They let me get into the streams to cool and rest from our hike. I was happy when we stopped for lunch, and Jacob held my bowl in front of me so I would eat my lunch and bones. By the time we got back to the apartment, I was tired. So, I climbed into my favorite chair, curled, and slept for a few hours. Five to six miles is a long way for a ten-year-old dog to hike! Mark's friends left, but returned for dinner.

Five days later, more of Mark's friends came to visit: Bill and Kathy. They arrived on a late afternoon. After dinner, we went for a walk on the road. The next day we went hiking along Rough and Tumble Creek in the Buffalo Peaks Wilderness. After we stopped for lunch, all I did was drink some water. I didn't want any of the food that Mark brought. After another five- to six-mile hike, Mark let me get into the South Platte River for a while. How great that cold water felt on my hot skin! He took a small towel and dried me off before I got into the Jeep. After we got back to the apartment, everyone rested. I climbed into my chair and slept for part of the afternoon. That evening I did eat all my dinner. My diarrhea was gone.

Since Mark had given Bill and Kathy the big bed and bedroom, he had been sleeping on the sofa/futon and I had been sleeping in my chair. After they left, we returned to our bed and bedroom. We slept late, got up, went for walk, and ate breakfast. Then, as Mark had been telling me all week, he gave me a bath in the bathtub. After he got me into it, he let water run into it, whetted me, soaped me, rinsed me, and dried me with a large gray towel. Not only did I smell good, but I felt good. I was happy! I wanted to play!

For the next few days we slept later than usual. Then, we would walk so I could pee and poop. I refused to take my medicine, but Mark wrapped it in soft dog food, and he wouldn't leave me alone until I took it out of a small bowl. Most mornings I didn't eat any breakfast.

On Saturday afternoon, August 14, 2022, Mark took me to the old town of Fairplay. We walked around the history display, seeing the locomotive engine, a few cars, and a caboose and lots of old log buildings from the 1800 mining days. All of the shops Mark wanted to browse let me in. Some proprietors talked to me, and one gave me treats and a bowl of water. All I wanted to do was to smell the grass growing in between shops or along the sidewalk and pee on it!

The next day Mark decided to take us hiking again. We stopped at a car park on Park Co. 18 and hiked the trail for four- to six-miles. We turned around when the trail began to go down the mountain. After turning around, we stopped to eat; all I wanted was a bowl of water. We got back to the Jeep and headed back to the apartment. I was tired. So, I climbed into my chair and slept part of the afternoon. At dinner time I ate all my food. The next day I was very tired.

A few days later, Mark took me hiking again on a three- to four-mile walk on the Limber Grove Trail at the Horseshoe Campground off of Park Co. 18—about seven miles in on that rugged, pot-holed, washboard road!

With me in the lead, we hiked through bristlecone pine trees. At the rock-slide, we turned around because I was getting tired and Mark was concerned about me hurting my foot or breaking a leg on the loose scree. We got back to our apartment around 1 p.m., ate lunch, and both of us napped. The next day Mark had to bribe me with a few morsels of cooked chicken or lasagna to get me to eat my food and to take my medicine. One of my favorite people, Matthew, came to visit us, and all of us went hiking on the Rough and Tumble Trail in the Buffalo Peaks Wilderness. Matthew took my leash, and that made me very happy. Also, I got to get into the South Platte River upon our return to the trailhead. While Mark fixed brunch for Matthew and himself, I climbed into my chair in the apartment and napped.

Near the end of August, during our last week in the apartment, I awakened from my nap in my chair around 4 p.m., stretched, and began to cry, squeal, yawn, etc. I had been asleep on my left leg, and it had either gone to sleep or was having a muscle spasm, when I stretched, and it hurt. At first I began to lick my left paw, but then I decided to get out of the chair and lie on the floor and lick it there. At dinner time, I took my medicine, ate my supper, and went back to my chair. However, I got hot in the afternoon sun shining through the window. So, I jumped out of the chair, lay on the rug on my side, and took my post-dinner nap.

Often during our time in the apartment in Colorado Mark told me that he considered it to be a privilege to sleep next to me. I know he could feel me move during the night, and he often took my blanket and covered me after I settled.

One morning we walked down the steps and out to the driveway to begin our walk to the main gravel road, and there stood an old bull moose with huge antlers in velvet. I had never seen a moose before; he was large. When he spotted Mark and me, he walked slowly down the lane as far as the woodpile, turned right, and slipped away into the woods. Later that same evening, when Mark was getting read to wash dishes after dinner, he called me to look out the double windows behind my chair, and there was the bull moose again, listening to the evening news from the TV! I got all excited upon seeing him again, growled a little, and watched as he walked into the woods.

Then, our time in Fairplay came to an end. I watch Mark gather our things and pack the Jeep on the day before we left. On September 1, we headed home at 7 a.m. Mark drove all day, stopping only one time at a rest area so we could eat lunch. We stayed at the Evergreen Motel outside Pratt,

Kansas. I like that motel because there is a park in the front for Mark to walk me; there I can see cars passing on the highway and smell all kinds of things. I ate my food and took my medicine that evening. The next day we left at 6:45 a.m. in the fog. When we got to Parsons, Kansas, we ran into rain, which continued until we got outside of Springfield. On Interstate 44, the eighteen-wheelers continued to drive seventy or more miles per hour, even though no one could see the line in the highway. Nevertheless, Mark was cautious, and got us home at 12:30 p.m. I was happy to be home, but I did enjoy all the adventures of the month of August.

EPILOGUE

Now that I have entered firmly into my tenth of human years and my sixty-seventh of dog years, I'm hoping to live another three to five human years which will make me anywhere from sixty-seven to ninety-three. With the proper medical attention, the right drugs, and a balanced diet I may get there. What I know at this point in my life is that Mark is doing all he can to keep me healthy, and I show him how much I love him with kisses, dances, and greetings.

I like to roll in sawdust and mulch. I love to explore garages. I like to watch cars and trucks, and I like to ride in a car or truck. I don't like getting hot or getting wet in the rain. I do like getting cool in a cold stream of water or pool. I express myself by raising my eyebrows and raising and lowering my ears! I like to play with duckie and clean him/her. I like to tear apart cloth bones, remove the stuffing and squeaker toy in it, and pile the stuffing on either side of me. I like to clean my legs—front and back—like a cat and wash my face like a cat after wetting my legs. I like to sleep with my head on the edge of the bed or the ends of steps. When I am bored (that is, when my walk is interrupted through discussion with another person and Mark), I eat grass. I like to rub my back against furniture, walls, the bed, etc. When I am hot, I find a cool spot on the floor and lie spread eagle on it. I like to catch flies and bees and eat them. Often, I eat while lying spread eagle on the floor. I can be very stubborn and refuse to come or to do what I am told or asked to do. I like to wear my bandanas, coat, and snow booties, and I like to be covered with my blanket at night. I like to receive a few bites of food from Mark's plate in my bowl, once we sit down to eat.

I have written this book for humans, who have dogs. I want the humans to know that what they do or don't do to, for, with their dog affects the dog for life. After I was taken away from my mother and placed in a home where I was abused, I was left with abandonment anxiety. I was left alone in the house and left alone outside the house, often in the thunder, lightning, rain, sleet, snow, etc. After four years, I was abandoned to two shelters. After I was rescued, I was abandoned to Mark, whom I trust not to ever abandon me again. However, to this day, when Mark leaves the house without me, my abandonment anxiety returns and haunts me until he returns. "I'll be back in an hour," he tells me, but I find it so hard to trust that he will, even though he has always returned to take care of me!

Dogs, no matter how vicious we appear to be, have physical and psychological feelings. We get hurt when we are hit, beaten, kicked, slapped, tugged, etc. We get hungry when we are not fed. We get thirsty when the water is not replenished in our bowl. We get hurt when we are ignored, criticized, severely reprimanded, overly punished. We love to learn what our owner's expect of us; we just have to be taught how to sit, stay, roll, stop, fetch, etc. Play comes naturally when we desire to return the love we receive. We take great pride in being with those humans who get to know us.

The greatest joy I have is that Mark knows me. He knows my good traits and he knows my bad traits, and he accepts me for the free spirit I am. I know he loves me because he demonstrates it every day by taking me for walks, feeding me, giving my medicine to me, spending time talking with me, petting me and giving me belly rubs, playing with me, visiting me on the front porch, and tucking me into bed at night. He takes me with him on long trips. His showering of love upon me evokes my showering of love upon him. We communicate through mutual love, and that communication is enshrined in the words of this book. If you take to heart these words by applying them to your dog, you will be enriched for the rest of your life. You will get to know your dog as dog, and he or she will get to know you as human.

Recent Books by Mark G. Boyer published by Wipf & Stock

Nature Spirituality: Praying with Wind, Water, Earth, Fire

A Spirituality of Ageing

Weekday Saints: Reflections on Their Scriptures

Human Wholeness: A Spirituality of Relationship

A Simple Systematic Mariology

Praying Your Way through Luke's Gospel and the Acts of the Apostles

An Abecedarian of Animal Spirit Guides: Spiritual Growth through Reflections on Creatures

Overcome with Paschal Joy: Chanting through Lent and Easter—Daily Reflections with Familiar Hymns

Taking Leave of Your Home: Moving in the Peace of Christ

An Abecedarian of Sacred Trees: Spiritual Growth through Reflections on Woody Plants

Divine Presence: Elements of Biblical Theophanies

Fruit of the Vine: A Biblical Spirituality of Wine

Names for Jesus: Reflections for Advent and Christmas

Talk to God and Listen to the Casual Reply: Experiencing the Spirituality of John Denver

Christ Our Passover Has Been Sacrificed: A Guide through Paschal Mystery Spirituality—Mystical Theology in The Roman Missal

Rosary Primer: The Prayers, The Mysteries, and the New Testament

From Contemplation to Action: The Spiritual Process of Divine Discernment Using Elijah and Elisha as Models

Love Addict

All Things Mary: Honoring the Mother of God—An Anthology of Marian Reflections

Shhh! The Sound of Sheer Silence: A Biblical Spirituality that Transforms

What is Born of the Spirit is Spirit: A Biblical Spirituality of Spirit

Very Short Reflections—for Advent and Christmas, Lent and Easter, Ordinary Time, and Saints—through the Liturgical Year

Living Parables: Today's Versions

My Life of Ministry, Writing, Teaching, and Traveling: The Autobiography of an Old Mines Missionary

300 Years of the French in Old Mines: A Narrative History of the Oldest Village in Missouri

Journey into God: Spiritual Reflections for Travelers

Monthly Entries for the Spiritual but no Religious through the Year: Texts, Reflections, Journal/Meditations, and Prayers for the SBNR

www.ingramcontent.com/pod-product-compliance
Lightning Source LLC
Chambersburg PA
CBHW051144020726
47501CB00005B/1664